A CINDERELLA FOR THE GREEK

BY

JULIA JAMES

MILLS
BOON

First published in Great Britain 2016
By Mills & Boon, an imprint of HarperCollins*Publishers*
1 London Bridge Street, London, SE1 9GF

Large Print edition 2017

© 2016 Julia James

ISBN: 978-0-263-07057-6

Printed and bound in Great Britain
by CPI Antony Rowe, Chippenham, Wiltshire

A CINDERELLA
FOR THE GREEK

To my younger self.

CHAPTER ONE

MAX VASILIKOS LOWERED his tall frame into the leather chair by the desk and relaxed back into it, his long legs stretching out in front of him.

'OK, what have you got for me?'

His UK agent handed him a set of glossy brochures. 'I think there are some good contenders here, Mr Vasilikos,' he said hopefully to this most demanding of clients.

Max's dark eyes glanced briefly, and then he found his gaze lingering on only one of the properties.

An English country house, in warm honey-coloured stone, with wisteria tumbling over the porch, surrounded by verdant gardens and sheltering woodland, with a glimpse of a lake beyond the lawn. Bathed in sunshine, the whole place had an appeal that held his gaze, making him want to see the real thing.

He picked up the brochure and shifted his gaze to his agent.

'This one,' he said decisively.

Ellen paused in the hallway. She could hear her stepmother's sharp voice coming from the drawing room.

'This is exactly what I've been hoping for! And I will *not* have that wretched girl trying to spoil it—again!'

'We've just *got* to hurry up and sell this place!'

The second voice came from Ellen's stepsister Chloe, petulant and displeased.

Ellen's mouth tightened. She was all too aware of the source of their displeasure. When Pauline had married Ellen's widowed father she and her daughter Chloe had had only one aim—to spend his money on the luxury lifestyle they craved for themselves. Now all that was left, after years of their lavish spending, was the house they had jointly inherited with Ellen after her father's sudden death last year from a heart attack—and they couldn't wait to sell it. That it was Ellen's home, and had been in her family for generations, bothered them not in the slightest.

Their hostility towards her was nothing new. From the moment they'd invaded her life Pauline and her daughter had treated Ellen with complete contempt. How could Ellen—tall and ungainly, clumping around 'like an elephant', as they always described her—possibly compare with slender, petite and oh-so-pretty Chloe?

She clumped down the rest of the stairs deliberately now, to drown out their voices. It sounded, she thought grimly, as if her stepmother had hopes of a potential purchaser for Haughton. Despite knowing she would need to resort to legal action against her stepdaughter in order to force a sale through, Pauline obdurately kept the house on the market, and relentlessly went on at Ellen to try to wear down her resistance and force her to agree to sell up.

But Ellen's heart had steeled in that first winter without her father, when her stepmother and Chloe had been disporting themselves expensively in the Caribbean. She would make it as difficult as she could for Pauline to sell her beloved home—the home Ellen had been happy in until the terrible day her mother had been killed in a car crash, sending her father spiralling into a grieving tailspin of loneliness that had made him so dangerously vulnerable to entrapment by Pauline's avaricious ambitions.

As Ellen walked into the drawing room two pairs of ice-blue eyes went to her, their joint expressions openly hostile.

'What kept you?' Pauline demanded immediately. 'Chloe texted you an hour ago saying that we needed to talk to you.'

'I was taking lacrosse practice,' Ellen returned, keeping her tone even. She sat down heavily on an armchair.

'You've got mud on your face,' Chloe informed her sneeringly.

Her gaze was not just hostile, but contemptuous. Ellen could see why. Her stepsister was wearing one of her countless designer outfits— a pair of immaculately cut trousers with a cashmere knit top—her nails were newly manicured and varnished, her freshly cut and styled ash-blonde hair and make-up perfect.

A familiar silent sigh went through Ellen. Chloe was everything she was not! Petite, with a heart-shaped face, and so, *so* slim! The contrast with her own appearance—she was still wearing the coaching tracksuit from the nearby private girls' school where she taught Games and Geography, with her thick, unmanageable hair gripped back in a bushy ponytail and her face devoid of any make-up except the streak of mud on her cheek that Chloe had so kindly pointed out!—was total.

'The estate agents phoned this afternoon,' Pauline opened, her gimlet eyes on Ellen. 'There's been another expression of interest—'

'And we don't want *you* ruining things!' broke in Chloe waspishly, throwing a dagger look at her stepsister. 'Especially with this guy,' she continued.

There was a note in her voice that caught Ellen's attention. So, too, did the discernibly smug expression in Pauline's eyes.

'Max Vasilikos is looking for a new addition to his portfolio—he thinks Haughton might be it.' Pauline elucidated.

Ellen looked blank, and Chloe made a derisive noise. 'Oh, for heaven's sake, don't expect *her* to know who Max Vasilikos is,' she said. 'Max Vasilikos,' she spelt out to Ellen, 'is a stinking rich property tycoon. He's also just had an affair with Tyla Brentley—you *must* have heard of her, at least?'

Ellen had, as a matter of fact. She was an English actress who'd found fame in Hollywood in a hugely successful romantic blockbuster, and the pupils at her school were full of her. But as for this Max Vasilikos... Apart from surmising that with a name like that he must be of Greek origin—well, 'stinking rich' property tycoons were nothing to do with her.

And they would be nothing to do with Haughton either, please God! A cold shiver went down her spine. Someone like this Max Vasilikos would sell it on for a huge profit to a Russian oligarch or a Middle Eastern sheikh who would spend a week or two in it, at best, every year or so. And it would languish, unloved and unlived-in...

Pauline was speaking again. 'Max Vasilikos is sufficiently interested to come and view the property himself. As a courtesy I have invited him to lunch with us.'

That smug expression was in her eyes again. Ellen just looked at her. 'Does he understand the ownership structure of Haughton and that I am unwilling to sell my share?' she asked bluntly.

Pauline waved a hand to brush aside this unpalatable detail. 'What *I* understand, Ellen,' she said bitingly, 'is that if—*if*—he expresses an interest, we will be very, very fortunate. I do *not*,' she emphasised, 'want *you* rocking the boat. Moreover—' she glared at her stepdaughter '—if nothing I can say will make you see sense about selling up, perhaps Max Vasilikos can.'

There was an explosive, choking half-laugh from Chloe. 'Oh, Mummy, don't,' she jeered. 'You simply *can't* inflict *her* on him!'

Ellen felt the jibe, flinching inwardly and yet knowing it for nothing but the truth. No man—let alone one who dated film stars—could look at her with anything but complete indifference to her appearance. She had nothing to attract a man in her looks. Knew it...accepted it. At least, though, she wasn't cruel like her stepsister.

Pauline had turned to Chloe. 'Nevertheless, that's just what we are going to have to do,' she continued. 'Ellen *has* to be there.' Her gaze went back to her stepdaughter. 'We'll present a united front.'

Ellen stared. United? A more fractured family was hard to imagine. But, although it would

be gruelling to endure, it would at least, she realised grimly, give her the opportunity to make
it clear to this Max Vasilikos just how unwilling
she was to sell her share of her home.

With reluctant acquiescence she got to her feet.
She needed a shower, and she was hungry, too.
She headed for the kitchen. It was the part of the
house she liked best now—the former servants'
quarters, and the perfect place for keeping out
of Pauline and Chloe's way. Cooking was not a
priority for either woman.

She'd moved her bedroom to one of the back
rooms as well, overlooking the courtyard at the
rear of the house, and adapted an adjacent room
for her own sitting room. She ventured into the
front part of the house as little as possible—but
now, as she headed back across the hall to the
green baize door that led to the servants' quarters,
she felt her heart squeeze as she gazed around her
at the sweeping staircase, the huge stone fireplace,
the massive oak doorway, the dark wood panelling and the ancient flagstones beneath her feet.

How she loved this house. Loved it with a
strong, deep devotion. She would never willingly
relinquish it. *Never!*

* * *

Max Vasilikos slowed the powerful car as the road curved between high hedges. He was deep in Hampshire countryside bright with early spring sunshine, and almost at his destination. He was eager to arrive—keen to see for himself whether the place that had so immediately appealed to him in the estate agency's photos would live up to his hopes. And not just from an investment perspective. The encircling woods and gardens, the mellow stonework, the pleasing proportions and styling of the house all seemed—*homely.* That was the word that formed in his mind.

In fact... *It's a house I could see myself in—*

The thought was in his head before he could stop it, and that in itself was cause for surprise. He'd always been perfectly happy to live a globe-trotting life, staying in hotels or serviced apartments, ready to board a plane at any moment.

But then, he'd never known a home of his own. His eyes shadowed. His mother had always been ashamed of his illegitimacy, and that was why, Max thought bleakly, she'd married his step-father—to try and disguise her child's father-less status.

But the very last thing his stepfather had wanted was to accept his wife's bastard into his family. All he'd wanted was a wife to be a skivvy, an unpaid drudge to work in his restaurant in a little tourist town on a resort island in the Aegean. Max had spent his childhood and teenage years helping her, keeping the *taverna* going while his stepfather played host to his customers, snapping his fingers at Max to wait at tables while his mother cooked endlessly.

The day his mother had died—of exhaustion as much as the lung disease that had claimed her—Max had walked out, never to return. He'd taken the ferry to Athens, his eyes burning not just with grief for his mother's death, but with a fierce, angry determination to make his own way in the world. And make it a glittering way. Nothing would stop him. He would overcome all obstacles, with determination driving him ever onwards.

Five years of slog in the construction industry and finally he'd saved enough from his wages to make his first property purchase—a derelict farmhouse that, with the sweat of his brow, he'd restored and sold to a German second-home-owner, making enough profit to buy two more properties. And so it had begun. The Vasilikos property empire had snowballed into the global enterprise it now was. His tightened mouth twisted into a caustic smile of ruthless satisfaction. It even included his stepfather's *taverna*—picked up for a song when his stepfather's idleness had bankrupted him.

Max's expression changed abruptly as his satnav indicated that he'd arrived at his destination. Manoeuvring between two large, imposing stone gate pillars, he headed slowly along a lengthy drive flanked by woodland and massed rhododendrons that in turn gave way to a gravelled carriage sweep alongside the frontage of the house. He slowed down, taking in the vista in front of him, feeling satisfaction shaping inside him.

The photos hadn't deceived—everything they'd promised was here. The house was nestled into its landscaped grounds, the mellow stonework a warm honey colour, and sunshine glanced off the mullioned windows. The stone porch with its gnarled oak door was flanked by twisted wisteria, bare at this time of year, but with the promise of the show to come. Already in bloom, however, were ranks of golden daffodils, marching thickly along the herbaceous borders on either side of the porch.

Max's sense of satisfaction deepened. It looked good—more than good. Not too large, not too grand, but elegant and gracious, and steeped in the long centuries of its existence. An English country house, yes, built for landowners and gentry, but also inviting, its scale domestic and pleasing. More than a grand house—a *home*.

Could it become my home? Could I see myself living here?

He frowned slightly. Why was he thinking such things?

Have I reached the age where I'm starting to think of settling down? Is that it?

Settling down? That was something he'd never thought of with any woman—certainly not with Tyla. She was like him: rootless, working all over the world.

Maybe that's why we suited each other—we had that in common.

Well, even if that had been true enough at the time, it hadn't been sufficient to stop him ending things with her. Her absorption in her own beauty and desirability had become tiresome in the end—and now she was busy beguiling her latest leading man, a Hollywood A-lister. Max wished her well with it.

So maybe I need a new relationship? Maybe I'm in search of novelty? Something different—?

He gave himself a mental shake. He wasn't here to ponder his private life. He was here to make a simple business decision—whether to buy this property or not for his extensive portfolio.

Engaging gear again, he crunched forward over the gravel, taking the car around to the back of the house. He drew to a halt and got out of the car, again liking what he saw. The rear façade, built as servants' quarters, might not have the elegance of the front section of the house, but the open cobbled courtyard was attractive, bordered by outhouses on two sides and prettied up with tubs of flowers, and a wooden bench positioned in the sunshine by the kitchen door.

His approval rating of the house went up yet another notch. He strolled towards the door, to ask if it was okay to leave his car there, but just as he was about to knock it was yanked open, and someone hefting a large wooden basket and a bulging plastic bin bag cannoned straight into him.

A Greek expletive escaped him and he stepped back, taking in whoever had barged so heavily into him. She was female, he could see, and though she might be categorised as 'young' she had little else that he could see to recommend her to his sex. She was big, bulky, with a mop of dark bushy hair yanked back off her face into some kind of ponytail. She wore a pair of round glasses on her nose and her complexion was reddening unbecomingly. The dark purple tracksuit she wore was hideous, and she looked distinctly overweight, Max decided.

Despite her unprepossessing appearance, not for a moment did Max neglect his manners.

'I'm so sorry,' he said smoothly. 'I was seeking to enquire whether I might leave my car here.' He paused. 'I *am* expected. Max Vasilikos to see Mrs Mountford.'

The reddening female dragged her eyes from him and stared at his car, then back at him. Her cheeks flushed redder than ever. She shifted the weight of the basket on her hip but did not answer him.

'So, *is* it all right to leave my car here?' Max prompted.

With visible effort the woman nodded. She might have mumbled something as well, but whatever it was it was indistinct.

He gave a swift, courtesy-only smile. 'Good,' he said, dismissing her from his notice, and turned away to head around the house to the front entrance, his gaze sweeping out over the gardens as he walked. Even this early in the spring he could see that they would be beautiful as summer arrived.

Again he felt that unexpected sense of approval that was nothing to do with whether or not this place would be a profitable investment to make. He walked up to the front door—a massive, studded oak construction—hoping the interior of the house would match the charms of the exterior.

The door opened in front of him—clearly his arrival had been communicated. The female standing there could not, Max thought, have been more different from the one who'd cannoned into him at the kitchen door. She was petite, ultra-slender and immaculately styled, from her chic ash-blonde hair and perfect make-up to her well-tailored outfit whose pale blue hue matched the colour of her eyes. The fragrance of an expensive perfume wafted from her as she smiled warmly at him.

'Mr Vasilikos—do come in!'

She stood back as Max walked in, taking in a large hall with a flagged stone floor, a cavernous fireplace, and a broad flight of stairs leading upwards. It suited the house, Max thought.

'I'm Chloe Mountford. I'm *so* glad you could come.' The daughter of the house—as he assumed she must be—was gliding towards one of the sets of double doors opening off the hall, and she threw them open with a dramatic gesture as he followed after her.

'Mummy, it's Mr Vasilikos,' she announced.

Mummy? Max reminded himself that it was common in English upper crust circles for adult children to use such a juvenile form of address for their parents. Then he walked into the room. It was a double aspect drawing room, with another large but more ornate marble fireplace and a lot of furniture. The decor was pale grey and light blue, and it was clear to his experienced eyes that a top-class interior designer had been let loose in there.

He found himself conscious of a feeling of disappointment—it was all just *too* perfect and calculatedly tasteful—and wondered what the original decor would have looked like. The effect now was like something out of a highly glossy upmarket magazine.

I couldn't live in this. It's far too overdone. I'd have to change it—

The thought was in his head automatically, and he frowned slightly. He was getting ahead of himself again.

'Mr Vasilikos, how lovely to meet you.'

The slim, elegant woman greeting him from one of the upholstered sofas by the fire, holding out a diamond-ringed hand to him, was extremely well preserved and, like her daughter, had clearly lavished money on her clothes and her appearance. A double rope of pearls adorned her neck which, Max suspected, had benefitted from the attentions of a plastic surgeon at some time.

'Mrs Mountford.' Max greeted the widowed owner, his handshake firm and brief, then sat himself down where she indicated, at the far end of the sofa opposite, away from the fire. Chloe Mountford settled herself prettily on a third sofa, facing the fire, at the end closest to Max.

'I'm delighted to welcome you to Haughton,' Mrs Mountford was saying now, in a smiling, gracious tone.

Max smiled politely in response as her daughter took up the conversational baton.

'Thank you for taking the time from what I'm sure must be a dreadfully busy schedule. Are you in England long this visit, Mr Vasilikos?' she asked brightly.

'My plans are fluid at the moment,' Max returned evenly. He found himself wondering whether Chloe Mountford was likely to make a play for him. He hoped not. The current fashion might be for ultra-thin figures, but they were not to his taste. Nor, of course, were women at the other extreme.

His mind flickered back to the female who'd cannoned into him at the back door. Being overweight wasn't a good look either—especially when a woman was badly dressed and plain to boot. A flicker of pity went through him for any woman so sadly unattractive. Then Chloe Mountford was speaking again.

'There speaks the globetrotting tycoon!' she said with a light laugh.

She turned her head expectantly as a door set almost invisibly into the papered wall opened abruptly and a bulky frame carrying a loaded coffee tray reversed into the room. It belonged, Max could see instantly, to the very female he'd just been mentally pitying for her lack of physical appeal.

The unlovely tracksuit had been swapped for a grey skirt and a white blouse, the trainers replaced with sturdy lace-up flats, but her hair was still caught back in a style-less bush, and the spectacles were still perched on her nose. She made her way heavily into the room, looking decidedly awkward, Max could see.

'Ah, Ellen, there you are!' exclaimed Pauline Mountford as the coffee tray was set down on the low table by the fireside. Then his hostess was addressing him directly. 'Mr Vasilikos, this is my stepdaughter, Ellen.'

Max found his assumptions that the hefty female was some kind of maid rearranging themselves. Stepdaughter? He'd been unaware of that—but then, of course, knowing the details of the family who owned Haughton was hardly relevant to his decision whether to purchase it or not.

'How do you do?' he murmured as he politely got to his feet.

He saw her face redden as she sat herself down heavily on the sofa beside Chloe Mountford. Max's glance, as he seated himself again, went between the two young women sitting on the same sofa, took in the difference between the two females graphically. They could hardly be a greater contrast to each other—one so petite and beautifully groomed, the other so large and badly presented. Clearly nothing more than step-sisters, indeed.

'Mr Vasilikos,' the stepdaughter returned briefly, with the slightest nod of her head. Then she looked across at her stepmother. 'Would you like me to pour? Or do *you* want to be mother?' she said.

Max heard the bite in her voice as she addressed the owner of the house and found himself sharpening his scrutiny.

'Please do pour, Ellen, dear,' said Mrs Mountford, ignoring the distinctly baiting note in her stepdaughter's tone of voice.

'Cream and sugar, Mr Vasilikos?' she asked, looking straight at him.

There was a gritty quality to her voice, as if she found the exchange difficult. Her colour was still heightened, but subsiding. Her skin tone, distinctly less pale than her stepsister's carefully made up features, definitely looked better when she wasn't colouring up, Max decided. In fact, now he came to realise it, she had what might almost be described as a healthy glow about her—as if she spent most of her time outside. Not like the delicate hothouse plant her stepsister looked to be.

'Just black, please,' he answered. He didn't particularly want coffee, let alone polite chit-chat, but it was a ritual to be got through, he acknowledged, before he could expect a tour of the property that he was interested in.

He watched Pauline Mountford's sadly unlovely stepdaughter pour the coffee from a silver jug into a porcelain cup and hand it to him. He took it with a murmur of thanks, his fingers inadvertently making contact with hers, and she grabbed her hand back as if the slight touch had been an unpleasant electric shock. Then she ferociously busied herself pouring the other three cups of coffee, handing them to her stepmother and sister, before sitting back with her own and stirring it rapidly.

Max sat back, crossing one leg over the other, and took a contemplative sip of his coffee. Time to get the conversation going where he wanted it to go.

'So,' he opened, with a courteous smile of interest at Pauline Mountford, 'what makes you wish to part with such a beautiful property?'

Personally, he might think the decor too overdone, but it was obviously to his hostess's taste, and there was no point in alienating her. Decor could easily be changed—it was the house itself he was interested in.

And he *was* interested—most decidedly so. That same feeling that had struck him from the first was strengthening all the time. Again, he wondered why.

Maybe it's coming from the house itself?

The fanciful idea was in his head before he could stop it, making its mark.

As he'd spoken he'd seen Pauline Mountford's stepdaughter's coffee cup jerk in her grip and her expression darken. But his hostess was replying.

'Oh, sadly there are too many memories here! Since my husband died I find them too painful. I know I must be brave and make a new life for myself now.' She gave a resigned sigh, a catch audible in her voice. 'It will be a wrench, though...' She shook her head sadly.

'Poor Mummy.' Her daughter reached her hand across and patted her mother's arm, her voice warm with sympathy. Chloe Mountford looked at him. 'This last year's been just dreadful,' she said.

'I'm sorry for your loss,' Max murmured. 'But I can understand your reasons for wishing to sell.'

A sharp clunk came from the sofa opposite, and his eyes flicked to see his hostess's stepdaughter had dropped her coffee cup on to its saucer. Her expression, he could tell, was tight. His focus sharpened. Beneath his swift glance in her direction he saw her cheeks redden again. Then she reached for the silver coffee pot and busied herself pouring another cup. She did not speak, but the tightness in her face was unabated, even as the colour started to ebb. She took a single gulp from the refilled cup, then abruptly got to her feet.

'I must go and see about lunch,' she said brusquely, pushing past the furniture to get to the service door.

As she left Pauline Mountford leant towards him slightly. 'Poor Ellen took my husband's death very hard,' she confided in a low voice. 'She was quite devoted to him.' A little frown formed on her well-preserved and, he suspected, well-Botoxed forehead. 'Possibly too much so...' She sighed.

Then her expression changed and she brightened.

'I'm sure you would like to see the rest of the house before lunch. Chloe will be delighted to take you on the grand tour!' she gave a light laugh.

Her daughter got to her feet and Max did likewise. He *was* keen to see the house—and not keen to hear any more about the personal circumstances of the Mountford family, which were of no interest to him whatsoever. Chloe Mountford might be too thin, and her stepsister just the opposite, but he found neither attractive. All that attracted him here was the house itself.

It was an attraction that the 'grand tour' only intensified. By the time he reached the upper floor, with its array of bedrooms opening off a long, spacious landing, and stood in the window embrasure of the master bedroom, gazing with satisfaction over the gardens to let his gaze rest on the reed-edged lake beyond, its glassy waters flanked by sheltering woodland, his mind was made up.

Haughton Court would be his. He was determined on it.

CHAPTER TWO

ELLEN MADE IT to the kitchen, her heart knocking. Having *anyone* arrive to look over her home, thinking he was going to buy it, was bad enough—but...oh, dear Lord...that it was such a man as Max Vasilikos! She felt her cheeks flame again, just as they'd flamed—horribly, hideously—in that first punishingly embarrassing moment of all but sending him flying at the back door.

She had been gawping like an idiot at the devastating male standing in front of her. Six foot plus, broad-shouldered, muscled, and just ludicrously good-looking, with classic 'tall dark stranger' looks and olive skin tones. Sable hair and charcoal eyes, a sculpted mouth, incised cheekbones and a jaw cut from the smoothest marble...

The impact he'd made had hit her all over again when she'd taken in the coffee. At least by then she'd been a fraction more prepared—prepared, too, for what she'd known would be the inevitable pitying glance he'd cast at her as she took her place beside Chloe.

She felt her throat tighten painfully. She knew exactly what he'd seen, and why he'd pitied her. She and Chloe couldn't have made a bigger contrast, sitting beside each other. Hadn't she seen that same expression countless times over the years, whenever male eyes had looked between the two of them? Chloe the svelte, lovely blonde—she the heavy, ungainly frump.

She wrenched her mind away from the image. She had more to concern her than her lack of looks. Somehow she was going to have to find an opportunity to lay it on the line for Max Vasilikos about his buying her home. Oh, Pauline and Chloe might trot out all that sickeningly hypocritical garbage about 'painful memories', but the truth was they couldn't wait to cash in on the sale of the last asset they could get their greedy hands on.

Well, she would defy them to the last.

They'll have to force it from me in a court of law, and I'll fight them every inch of the way. I'll make it the most protracted and expensive legal wrangle I can.

A man like Max Vasilikos—an investment purchaser who just wanted a quick sale and a quick profit—wouldn't want that kind of delay. So long as she insisted that she wouldn't sell, that he'd have to wait out a legal battle with Pauline and Chloe, she would be able to fend him off. He'd find somewhere else to buy—leave Haughton alone.

As she checked the chicken that was roasting, and started to chop up vegetables, that was the only hope she could hang on to.

He'll never persuade me to agree to sell to him. Never!

There was nothing Max could say or do that would make her change her mind. Oh, he might be the kind of man who could turn females to jelly with a single glance of his dark, dark eyes, but—her mouth twisted—with looks like hers she knew only too painfully she was the last female on the planet that a man like Max Vasilikos would bother to turn the charm on for.

'Sherry, Mr Vasilikos? Or would you prefer something stronger?' Pauline's light voice enquired.

'Dry sherry, thank you,' he replied.

He was back in the drawing room, his tour of the house complete, his mind made up. This was a house he wanted to own.

And to keep for his own use.

That was the most insistent aspect of his decision to purchase this place. Its prominence in his mind still surprised him, but he was increasingly getting used to its presence. The idea of having this place for himself—*to* himself. Mentally he let the prospect play inside his head, and it continued to play as he sipped at the proffered sherry, his eyes working around the elegant drawing room.

All the other rooms that Chloe had shown him bore the same mark of a top interior designer. Beautiful, but to his mind not authentic. Only the masculine preserve of the library had given any sense of the house as it must once have been, before it had been expensively made over. The worn leather chairs, the old-fashioned patterned carpets and the book-lined walls had a charm that the oh-so-tasteful other rooms lacked. Clearly the late Edward Mountford had prevented his wife from letting the designer into his domain, and Max could not but agree with that decision.

He realised his hostess was murmuring something to him and forced his attention back from the pleasurable meanderings of the way he would decorate this room, and all the others, once the house was his to do with as he pleased.

He was not kept making anodyne conversation with his hostess and her daughter for long, however. After a few minutes the service door opened again and Pauline Mountford's step-daughter walked in with her solid tread.

'Lunch is ready,' she announced bluntly.

She crossed to the double doors, throwing them open to the hall beyond. Despite her solidity she held herself well, Max noticed—shoulders back, straight spine, as if she were strong beneath the excess weight she must be carrying, if the way the sleeves of her ill-fitting blouse were straining over her arms was anything to go by. He frowned. It seemed wrong to him that his hostess and her daughter should be so elegantly attired, and yet Ellen Mountford—presumably, he realised, the daughter of the late owner—looked so very *in*elegant.

But then, sadly, he knew that so many women who felt themselves to be overweight virtually gave up on trying to make anything of what looks they had.

His gaze assessed her as he followed her into the dining room, her stepsister and stepmother coming in behind him.

She's got good legs, he found himself thinking. Shapely calves, at any rate. Well, that was something, at least! His eyes went to her thick mop of hair, whose style did nothing for her—it wouldn't have done anything for Helen of Troy, to his mind! A decent haircut would surely improve her?

As he took his seat at the end of the table, where she indicated, his eyes flicked over her face. The glasses, he decided, were too small for her, making her jaw look big and her eyes look small. And that was a shame, he realised, because her eyes were a warm sherry colour, with amber lights. He frowned again. Her lashes might be long— what he could see of them through her spectacle lenses—but that overgrown monobrow was *hideous*! Why on earth didn't she do something about it? Do something about the rest of her?

It wouldn't take that much, surely, to make her look better? Plus, of course, decent clothes that concealed her excess weight as much as possible. Best of all, however, would be for her to shift that weight. She should take more exercise, maybe.

And not eat so much...

Because as they settled into lunch it was clear to Max that he and Ellen Mountford were the only ones tucking in. That was a shame, because the roast chicken was delicious—the traditional 'Sunday lunch' that the English loved so much and did so well. But neither Pauline Mountford nor her daughter did anything more than pick at their food.

Max found himself annoyed. Didn't they realise that being too thin was as undesirable as the opposite? His eyes flickered to Ellen Mountford again. *Was* she overweight? Her blouse might be straining over her arms, but her jawline was firm, and there was no jowliness or softening under the chin.

She must have noticed him glancing at her, for suddenly he saw again that tide of unlovely colour washing up into her face. *That* most certainly did nothing for her. He drew his glance away. Why was he thinking about how to improve the appearance of Ellen Mountford? She was of no interest to him—how could she possibly be?

'What are your plans for the contents of the house?' he asked his hostess. 'Will you take the paintings with you when you sell?'

A sound that might have been a choke came from Ellen Mountford, and Max's eyes flicked back to her. The red tide had vanished, and now there was the same tightness in her face as he'd seen when her stepmother had mentioned her bereavement.

'Very possibly not,' Pauline Mountford was answering him. 'They do rather go with the house, do you not think? Of course,' she added pointedly, 'they would all need to be independently valued.'

Max's eyes swept the walls. He had no objection to having the artwork—or, indeed, any of the original furniture. The pieces that had been acquired via the interior designer were, however, dispensable. His gaze rested on an empty space on the wall behind Chloe Mountford, where the wallpaper was slightly darker.

'Sold,' said Ellen Mountford tersely. The look on her face had tightened some more.

Chloe Mountford gave a little laugh. 'It was a gruesome still life of a dead stag. Mummy and I hated it!'

Max gave a polite smile, but his gaze was on Chloe's stepsister. She didn't seem pleased about the loss of the dead stag painting. Then his attention was recalled by his hostess.

'Do tell us, Mr Vasilikos, where will you be off to next? Your work must take you all over the world, I imagine.' She smiled encouragingly at him as she sipped at her wine.

'The Caribbean,' he replied. 'I am developing a resort there on one of the lesser known islands.'

Chloe's pale blue eyes lit up. 'I *adore* the Caribbean!' she exclaimed enthusiastically. 'Mummy and I spent Christmas in Barbados last winter. We stayed at Sunset Bay, of course. There really isn't anything to compare, is there?' she invited, after naming the most prestigious resort on the island.

'It's superb in what it does,' Max agreed. The famous high-profile hotel was nothing like the resort *he* was developing, and the remote island was nothing like fashionable Barbados.

'Do tell us more,' invited Chloe. 'When will

the grand opening be? I'm sure Mummy and I would *love* to be amongst the very first guests.'

Max could see Ellen Mountford's expression hardening yet again with clear displeasure. He wondered at it. Out of nowhere, memory shafted like an arrow. His stepfather had been perpetually displeased by anything he'd ever said—so much that he'd learnt to keep his mouth shut when his stepfather was around.

He dragged his mind away from the unhappy memory, back to the present. 'Its style will be very different from Sunset Bay,' he said. 'The idea is for it to be highly eco-friendly, focussing on being self-sustaining. Rainwater showers and no air conditioning,' he elucidated, with a slight smile.

'Oh, dear...' Pauline shook her head regretfully. 'I don't think that would suit me. Too much heat is very trying, I find.'

'It won't be for everyone, I agree,' Max acknowledged tactfully. He turned towards Ellen. 'What do *you* think—would it attract you? Wood-built lodges open to the fresh air and meals cooked on open fires in the evenings?' He found himself unexpectedly wanting to draw her into the conversation, to hear her views. They would be different from her hothouse stepsister's, he was sure.

'Sounds like glamping,' she blurted in her abrupt manner.

Max's eyebrows drew together. 'Glamping?' he echoed, mystified.

'Glamorous camping. I believe that's the contraction it's for,' she elucidated shortly. 'Upmarket camping for people who like the idea of going back to nature but not the primitive reality of it.'

Max gave a wry smile. 'Hmm…that might be a good description for my resort,' he acknowledged.

A tinkling laugh came from Chloe. 'I'd say "glamorous camping" is a contradiction in terms! It would be luxury for Ellen, though—she runs camps for London kids. A million miles from upmarket. Totally basic.'

She gave a dramatic shudder, and Max heard the note of dismissal in her voice.

'Adventure breaks,' Ellen said shortly. 'The children enjoy it. They think it's exciting. Some of them have never been into the countryside.'

'Ellen's "good works"!' Pauline said lightly. 'I'm sure it's very uplifting.'

'And muddy!' trilled Chloe with a little laugh, and sought to catch Max's eye to get his agreement.

But Max's attention was on Ellen. It was unexpected to hear that she ran such breaks for deprived inner-city children, given her own privileged background. He realised that he was paying her more attention.

'Do you hold them here?' he asked interestedly.

If so, it was something he might keep on with—adding it to the extensive list of charitable enterprises that were his personal payback for the good fortune that had enabled him to attain the wealth he had.

'They're held at my school, nearby. We set up camp on the playing fields,' came the answer. 'That way the children can use the sports pavilion, including the showers, and have use of the swimming pool as well. So they get the fun of camping, plus the run of the facilities of a private school.'

As she spoke for the first time Max saw something light up in Ellen Mountford's eyes, changing her expression. Instead of the stony, closed look that alternated only with the tomato-red flaring of her cheeks when he paid her attention there was actually some animation, some enthusiasm. It made a significant difference to her features, he realised with surprise. They seemed lighter, somehow, less heavy, and not even those wretched spectacles could hide that.

Then, as if aware of his regard, he saw her face close down again and she grabbed at her wine glass, that telltale colour washing up into her face, destroying the transformation he'd started to glimpse. For some reason it annoyed him. He opened his mouth to make a reply, to ask another question, see whether he could get back that momentary animation, draw her out again. But his hostess was speaking now, and he had to turn his attention to her.

'After lunch,' said Pauline Mountford, 'I'm sure you would like to see the gardens here. It's a little early in the season as yet, but in a week or two the rhododendrons along the drive will start their annual show,' she told him smilingly. 'They are a blaze of colour!'

'Rhododendrons...' Max mused, more for something to say than anything else. 'Rose tree—that's the literal translation from the Greek.'

'How fascinating!' said Chloe. 'Do they come from Greece, then?'

'No. They come from the Himalayas.' Her step-sister's contradiction was immediate. 'The Victorians introduced them to England. Unfortunately they've taken over in some places, where they are invasive pests. '

Max saw her eyes flicker to Pauline and her daughter, her expression back to stony again.

Chloe, though, continued as if her stepsister had not spoken. 'And then a little later on in early summer we have the azaleas—they are absolutely gorgeous when they are fully out in May. Masses and masses of them! Mummy had the most beautiful walk created, that winds right through their midst—'

There was an abrupt clatter of silverware from her stepsister.

'No, she did *not*. The azalea walk has been there far longer. It was *my* mother who created it!'

The glare from behind Ellen Mountford's spectacle lenses was like a dagger, skewering the hapless Chloe as Max turned his head abruptly at the brusque interjection. Then his hostess's step-daughter scraped back her chair and got to her feet.

'If you've all finished—?' she said, and started to grab at the plates and pile them on the tray on the sideboard. She marched out with them.

As she disappeared Pauline Mountford gave a resigned sigh. 'Oh, dear,' she said. 'I do apologise for that.' She glanced at her daughter, who promptly took up the cue.

'Ellen can be so very…*sensitive,*' she murmured sadly. 'I should have known better.' She gave a little sigh of regret.

'We do our best,' her mother confirmed with another sad sigh. 'But, well…' She trailed off and gave a little shake of her head.

It *was* tricky, Max allowed, for his hostess and her daughter to have to smooth over the prickly behaviour of their step-relation, in which he was not interested, so he moved the conversation back to the topic he *was* interested in, asking how far Haughton was from the sea.

Chloe Mountford was just telling him that it would make an ideal base for Cowes Week, if sailing was an interest of his, when her stepsister made another entrance, bearing another tray weighed down with a large apple pie, a jug of custard and a bowl of cream, which she set down on the table heavily. She did not resume her place.

'I'll leave you to it,' she announced shortly. 'Coffee will be in the drawing room.'

Then she was gone, disappearing back through the service door.

'So, Mr Vasilikos, what do you make of Haughton?'

Pauline Mountford's enquiry was perfectly phrased, and accompanied by a charming smile. She was sitting in a graceful pose on the sofa in the drawing room, where they had repaired for the coffee that Ellen Mountford had so tersely informed them would be awaiting them.

Max had been the only one to partake of the apple pie—no surprise—but he was glad he had. It had been delicious—sweet pastry made with a very light touch indeed, and juicy apples spiced with cinnamon and nutmeg. Whoever had made it could certainly cook.

Had the graceless Ellen made it? If so, then whatever her lack of beauty she could certainly boast of *one* key asset to draw a man to her side. His thoughts ran on. But perhaps being a good cook was not to her personal advantage—not if she overindulged in her own creations.

He gave a little shake of his head. There he was, thinking about that woman again. *Why?* She was nothing to him, and would remain so. He relaxed back a fraction in his seat. His hostess was clearly fishing for whether he wanted to buy this place or not. Well, why not give her his good news right now? He'd made his decision—and every passing moment only confirmed it. It might have been a decision made on impulse, but it was a strong impulse—the strongest he'd ever had—and he was used to making decisions on the spot. His instinct had never failed him yet—and it would not fail him now.

'Charming,' he said decisively, stretching out his legs towards the fire in a fashion that was already proprietorial. 'I believe...' he bestowed a smile on her '...that we will be able to reach an agreement in the region of your asking price—which is a realistic one—subject, of course, to the usual considerations of purchase: a full structural survey and so forth.'

He saw her eyes light up, and from the corner of his eye he was sure that her daughter's had done the same.

'Oh, that is *excellent*!' came Pauline's gracious response.

'Marvellous!' echoed her daughter.

Enthusiasm was in her voice. And relief too— Max could detect that.

It did not surprise him. Being forced to live here with the perpetually prickly Ellen could hardly be comfortable. He did not blame either mother or daughter for being eager to make new lives for themselves. Or even, he allowed, for having preferred to be abroad this last year. Hadn't he himself hightailed it from his stepfather's *taverna* the moment his poor mother had been finally laid to rest?

He pulled his mind away again. He did not want to remember his miserable childhood and downtrodden mother. Nor was he interested in the tense convolutions of the Mountford family either.

He set down his empty cup. 'Before I leave,' he said, 'I'll take a look around the gardens and the outbuildings to the rear. No, don't get up—' This to Chloe, who had started to stand. He smiled. 'My footwear is more suitable for the outdoors than yours,' he explained, glancing at her stylish high heels and not adding that he preferred to keep his own pace, and would rather not have her endless panegyrics about the charms of a property he had already decided would be his.

Though it was only prudent to check out the areas he had not yet seen, he did not envisage there being anything so dreadful as to make him change his mind.

He strode from the room, and as he shut the door behind him he heard animated conversation break out behind him. To his ears it sounded... *jubilant*. Well, his own mood was just as buoyant. Satisfaction filled him, and a warm, proprietorial sense of well-being. He glanced around the hallway—soon to be *his* hallway.

He paused in his stride. A family had lived here for generations. Emotion kicked in him. It was an emotion he had never felt before, and one that startled him with its presence—shocked him even more with his certainty about it. The words were in his head, shaping themselves, taking hold. Taking root.

And now it will be my home—for my family.

The family of his own that he'd never had...the family he *would* have.

A pang stabbed at him. If his poor mother had survived longer how he would have loved to bring her here—make a home for her here, safe from the harshness of her life, cosseting her in the luxury he could now afford to bestow upon her.

But I'll do that for your grandchildren—give them the happy upbringing you could not give me—and I'll feel you smile and be glad! I've come a long way—a long, long way—and now I've found the place I want to call my home. I'll find the right woman for me and bring her here.

Who that woman would be he didn't know, but she was out there somewhere. He just had to find her. Find her and bring her here.

Home.

He started to walk forward again, heading for the baize door that led through to the back section of the house. He would check it out, then go out into the courtyard area, take a look at the outbuildings before making his way around to the gardens and exploring them.

He was just walking down the passageway towards the back door when a voice from the open doorway to what he could see was a large stone-flagged kitchen stopped him.

'Mr Vasilikos! I need to speak to you!'

He halted, turning his head. Ellen Mountford was standing there and her face was stony. Very stony indeed. Annoyance tensed him. He did not want this. He wanted to get outside and complete his inspection of the place.

'What about?' he replied with steely politeness.

'It's very important.'

She backed away, indicating that he should step into the kitchen.

Impatiently Max strode in, taking in an impression of a large room with old-fashioned wooden cupboards, a long scrubbed wooden table, a flagstone floor and a vast old-fashioned range cooker along one wall. The warmth from the oven enveloped him, and there was, he realised, a cosy, comfortable, lived-in feel to the space. No top interior designer had been let loose in here, that was for sure—and he was glad of it.

He turned his attention to Ellen Mountford. She'd taken up a position on the far side of the kitchen table and her hands were pressed down over the back of a chair. Tension was in every line of her body, and her expression was both stony and determined.

He frowned. *Now what?*

'There's something you have to know!'

The words burst from her, and he realised with a deepening of his frown that she was in a state of extreme agitation and nervousness.

He levelled his gaze at her. She seemed to be steeling herself after her dramatic outburst. 'And that is…?' he prompted.

He watched her take a gulping breath. Her cheeks seemed pale now—as pale as chalk. Not a trace of the colour that had so unflatteringly rushed there whenever he'd looked at her before.

'Mr Vasilikos, there's no easy way to tell you this, and for that I'm sorry, but you've had a completely wasted journey. Whatever my stepmother has led you to believe, Haughton is not for sale. And it never will be!'

CHAPTER THREE

MAX STILLED. THEN deliberately he let his gaze rest on her. 'Perhaps,' he said, and he made no effort to make his voice sound anything less than the way he intended it to sound—quelling—'you might like to explain what you mean by that.'

Ellen swallowed, had to force herself to speak. To say what she *had* to say. 'I own a third of Haughton and I have no wish to sell.'

Somehow she'd got the words out—but her heart was thumping like a hammer inside her. Ever since she'd rushed from the dining room, emotions storming, she'd been trying to nerve herself to find Max Vasilikos, get him away from Pauline and Chloe and tell him what she had to tell him. And now she'd done it—and he was not, it was obvious, taking it kindly.

His expression had steeled, and the dark brows were snapping together now. For a moment Ellen quailed. Up till now Max Vasilikos had, she realised belatedly, been playing the role of courteous, amenable guest. Now he was very different. A tough, powerful businessman who was hearing something he did not want to hear.

As she'd delivered her bombshell something had flickered in Max's mind at what she'd said, but it wasn't relevant for the moment.

His gaze rested on her. 'Why not?'

He saw her swallow again.

'What relevance does that question have?'

Max's expression changed. A moment ago it had looked formidable. Now there was a cynical cast to it. 'Perhaps you are holding out for a higher price,' he said.

Ellen's lips pressed together. 'I don't wish to sell Haughton—and I shan't.'

He looked at her for a moment. He looked neither quelling nor cynical. He seemed to be studying her, but she suddenly had the feeling that he'd retreated behind a mask.

'You do realise, do you not, that as only part-owner of this property if any of the other part-owners wish to sell they have the legal right to force such a sale?'

There was no colour in her face. Her cheekbones had whitened. Something moved in her eyes. Some deep emotion. He saw her jaw tense, her knuckles whiten over the chair-back.

'That would take months. I'd drag it out as long as I could. No purchaser would want that kind of costly delay.'

She would make that delay as long as possible, fight as hard as possible. *I won't roll over and give in!*

She felt sick with tension. Max Vasilikos's gaze rested on her implacably. Then, abruptly, his expression changed. His long lashes dipped down over his deep, dark and entirely inscrutable eyes.

'Well, be that as it may, Miss Mountford, I intend to view the rest of the property while I am here.'

She saw his glance go around the kitchen again, in an approving fashion.

'This is very pleasing,' he said. 'It's been left in its original state and is all the better for it.'

Ellen blinked. To go from defying him to agreeing with him confused her completely. 'My stepmother wasn't interested in doing up the kitchen quarters,' she said.

Max's eyes glinted. 'A lucky escape, then,' he said dryly.

There was a distinctly conspiratorial note to his voice, and Ellen's confusion deepened.

'You don't like the decor in the main house?' she heard herself saying, astonished. Surely property developers *loved* that full-blown interior-designed look?

Max smiled. 'Taste is subjective, and your stepmother's tastes are not mine. I prefer something less...contrived.'

'She's had it photographed for a posh interiors magazine!' Ellen exclaimed derisively, before she could stop herself.

'Yes, it would be ideal for such a publication,' he returned lightly. 'Tell me, is there anything left of the original furnishings and furniture?'

A bleak, empty look filled Ellen's face. 'Some of it was put up in the attics,' she said.

Any antiques or *objets d'art* of value that Pauline had not cared for had been sold—like the painting from the dining room and others she'd needed to dispose of so she and Chloe could go jaunting off on their expensive holidays.

'That's good to hear.' He nodded, making a

mental note to have the attic contents checked at some point. There were art valuations to get done, too, before the final sales contract was signed.

For signed it would be. His eyes rested now on the female who was so obdurately standing in the way of his intentions. Whatever her reasons, he would set them aside. Somehow she would be brought to heel. In all his years of negotiation, one thing he'd learnt for sure—there was always a way to get a deal signed and sealed. *Always.*

He wanted this place. Wanted it badly. More than he had ever thought to want any property... He wanted to make a home here.

He smiled again at the woman who thought so unwisely—so futilely!—to balk him of what he wanted. 'Well, I shall continue on my way, Miss Mountford. I'll see myself out—'

And he was gone, striding from the kitchen and down to the back door.

Ellen watched him go, her heart thumping heavily still, a feeling of sickness inside her. She heard the back door close as he went out. Words burned in her head, emotions churning.

Please let him leave! Leave and—and never come back!

Let him buy somewhere else—anywhere else. But leave me my home...oh, leave me my home!

Max stood in the shade of a tall beech tree overlooking the lake and took in the vista. It was good—all good. Everything about this place was good. He'd explored the outbuildings, realised they'd need work, but nothing too much, and mentally designated some of the old stables for his cars. He might keep some as stabling, too. He didn't ride, but maybe his children would like ponies one day.

He gave a half-laugh. Here he was, imagining children here before he'd even found the woman who would give them to him. Well, he'd have plenty of volunteers, that was for sure—not that he was keen on any of his current acquaintance. And his time with Tyla had been enjoyable, but their ways had parted. No, the woman he would bring here as his bride would be quite, quite different from the self-absorbed, vanity-driven film star bent on storming Hollywood. His chosen bride would be someone who would love this place as he would come to love it—love *him*, love their children...

He shook his head to clear his thoughts—he was running ahead of himself! First he had to buy this place. He frowned. The tripartite ownership structure should have been disclosed to him at the outset, not be delivered by bombshell. His frown deepened.

Well, that was a problem to ponder for later. Right now, he wanted to finish exploring the grounds beyond the formal gardens surrounding the house. He could see that a pathway ran through the long, unmown grass beside the sheltering woodland, around the perimeter of the reed-edged lake. He would walk along it and take a look at what he could see was a little folly on the far side.

My kids would love playing there—and we'd have picnics there in the summer. Maybe barbecues in the evening. Maybe swimming in the lake? I'll get a pool put in as well, of course—probably indoors, with a glass roof, given the English climate...

His thoughts ran on as he emerged from the shelter of the woodland. Then abruptly they cleared. He stared. There was someone over by the folly, leaning against the stonework. He watched as she straightened, and then set off along the path towards him. She was in running gear, he could see that from this distance, but not who it was. He frowned. If neighbours had got into the habit of using the place as a running track he'd better know about it—

Slowly he walked forward on an interception course. But as the runner approached him he felt the breath leave his body. Incredulity scissored through him.

It couldn't be! It just *couldn't*!

It could *not* be the sad, overweight, badly dressed frumpy female he'd pitied—impossible for it to be Ellen Mountford. Just *impossible*.

But it *was* her.

As the figure drew closer, its long, loping gait effortless and confident, his eyes were nailed to it. Tall, long-legged, with dark hair streaming behind like a flag, and a body…a body that was a total knockout—

It was impossible to tear his stunned gaze from her. From her strong, lithe body, perfectly contoured in a sports bra that moulded generous breasts, exposing not an inch of fat over bare, taut-waisted abs, with matching running shorts that hugged sleek hips, exposing the full length of her honed, toned quads.

Thee mou, she wasn't fat—she was *fit*. In both senses of the word! Fit and fabulous!

Every thought about her completely rearranged itself in his head. He could not take his eyes from her. He was in shock—and also something very different from shock. Something that sent the blood surging in his body.

Thanks to the sight of hers…

Greek words escaped his lips. Something about not believing his eyes, his senses, and something that was extreme appreciation of her fantastic physique. Then another thought was uppermost. *How did she hide that body from me?* At not one single point had there been the slightest indication of what she was hiding—and he hadn't noticed. Not for a moment, not for an instant! How had she done it?

But he knew—she'd done it by disguising that fantastic, honed, sleek, fit body of hers in those appalling clothes. In that unspeakable purple tracksuit that had turned her into some kind of inflated dummy, and that shapeless, ill-fitting grey skirt and even more shapeless and ill-fitting white blouse whose tightness of sleeve had had nothing whatsoever to do with her arms being fat—but had simply been because her biceps and triceps were honed, compacted muscle. He could see that now, as she approached more closely.

He stepped out from amongst the trees. 'Hello, there,' he said.

His greeting was affable, and pleasantly voiced, and it stopped her dead in her tracks as if a concrete block had dropped down in front of her from the sky.

Something that was partly a shriek of shock, partly a gasp of air escaped from Ellen. She stared, aghast—Max Vasilikos was the last person she wanted to see!

The emotional stress of the day, the agitation from having had to commandeer him and tell him she would never agree to sell her share of Haughton, had overset her so much that the moment he'd closed the back door behind him she'd headed upstairs to change into her running gear. She'd had to get out of the house. Had to work off the stress and tension and the biting anxiety. A long, hard run would help.

She'd set off on the long route, down the drive

and looping back through the woods, then into a field and back into the grounds, taking a breather by the folly before setting off around the lake, hoping against hope that by the time she got back to the house he and his flash car would have gone.

Instead here he was, appearing in front of her out of nowhere like the demon king in a pantomime!

A demon king in whose eyes was an expression that sent a wave of excruciating colour flooding through her.

She was agonisingly aware of her skimpy, revealing attire. Mercilessly revealing her muscular body. She lifted her chin, desperately fighting back her reaction. She would *not* be put out of countenance by him seeing her like this any more than she had been when he'd seen her plonked beside Chloe, and the dreadful contrast she'd made to her stepsister. It was a comparison that was hitting him again—she could see it as his eyes swept over her appraisingly.

'I could see you were totally different from Chloe—but not like *this*!' he exclaimed. 'You couldn't be more unalike—even sharing a surname, you'd never be taken for sisters in a thousand years.'

He shook his head in disbelief. Missing completely the sudden look of pain at his words in her eyes. Then he was speaking again.

'I'm sorry—I shouldn't be delaying you. Your muscles will seize up.' He started to walk forward in the direction of the house, his pace rapid, with long strides. 'Look,' he went on, 'keep going—but slow down to a jog so we can talk.'

He moved to one side of the path. She started up again, conscious that her heart was pounding far more quickly than the exertion of her run required. She found herself blinking. The casual cruelty of what he'd just said reverberated in her, but she must not let it show. With an effort, and still burningly conscious of her skimpy attire and perspiring body, of her hair held back only by a wide sweatband, of being bereft of the glasses she'd been wearing over lunch, she loped beside him.

'What about?' she returned. The thought came to her that maybe she could use this wretched encounter to convince him that there really was no point in his staying any longer—that buying Haughton was off the menu for him.

'I'm making an offer for this place,' he said, glancing at her. 'It will be near the asking price...' He trailed off.

Dismay lanced through her. 'I still don't want to sell my share,' she replied grittily.

'Your third...' Max didn't take his eyes from her '...will be well over a million pounds...'

'I don't care what it is. Mr Vasilikos—please understand—my share is not for sale at any price. I don't want to sell.'

'Why not?' His brows snapped together.

'What do you mean, why not?' she riposted. 'My reasons are my own—I don't want to sell.' She turned her face, making herself look at him. 'That's all there is to it. And I'll make it as hard as I possibly can for you to complete a sale. I'll fight it to the bitter end!'

Vehemence broke through in her voice and she could see it register with him. His eyebrows rose, and she knew he was about to say something— but she didn't want to hear. Didn't want to do anything but get away from him. Get back to the house, the sanctuary of her bedroom. Throw herself down on the bed and weep and weep. For what she feared most in the world would come true if this man went through with his threat!

She couldn't bear it—she just couldn't. She couldn't bear to lose her home. The place she loved most in all the world. *She couldn't bear it.*

With a burst of speed she shot forward, leaving him behind. Leaving behind Max Vasilikos, the man who wanted to wrench her home from her.

As he watched her power forward, accelerating away, Max let her go. But when she disappeared from sight across the lawns that crossed the front of the house his thoughts were full.

Why was Ellen Mountford so set on making difficulties for him? And why were his eyes following her fantastic figure until she was totally beyond his view? And why was he then regretting that she was beyond it?

The question was suddenly stronger in his head, knocking aside his concern about an easy purchase of the place he intended to buy, whatever obstacles one of its owners might put in his path.

When he reached the house Max went in search of his hostess. She was in the drawing room with her daughter, and both greeted him effusively, starting to ask him about his tour of the outbuildings and the grounds.

But he cut immediately to the chase.

'Why was I not informed of the ownership structure of this property?' he asked.

His voice was level, but there was a note in it that anyone who'd ever been in commercial negotiations with him would have taken as a warning not to try and outmanoeuvre him or prevaricate.

'Your stepdaughter apprised me of the facts after lunch,' he went on.

He kept his level gaze on Pauline. Beside her on the sofa, Chloe Mountford gave a little choke. An angry one. But her mother threw her a silencing look. Then she turned her face towards Max. She gave a little sigh.

'Oh, dear, what has the poor girl told you, Mr Vasilikos?' There was a note of apprehension in her voice.

'That she does not wish to sell her share,' he replied bluntly. 'And that she is prepared to force you to resort to legal measures to make her do so. Which will, as you must be aware, be both costly and time-consuming.'

Pauline Mountford's be-ringed fingers wound into each other. 'I'm so sorry, Mr Vasilikos, that you have been exposed to…well, to this, unfortunate development. I had hoped we could reach a happy conclusion between ourselves and—'

Max cut across her, his tone decisive. 'I make no bones that I want to buy this place,' he said. 'But I don't want problems and I don't want delays.'

'We don't either!' agreed Chloe promptly. 'Mummy, we've just *got* to stop Ellen ruining everything.'

He looked at the pair of them. 'Do you know what is behind her reluctance to sell?'

Pauline sighed again, her face shadowing. 'I believe,' she said slowly, 'that she is a very *unhappy* young woman. Poor Ellen has always found it very…*difficult*…to have us here.'

'She's hated us from the start,' Chloe said tightly. 'She's never made us welcome.'

Pauline sighed once more. 'Alas, I'm afraid it's true. She was at a difficult age when Edward married me. And I fear it is all too common, sadly, for a daughter who has previously had the undivided attention of her father not to allow that he might seek to find happiness with someone else. I did my best...' she sighed again '...and so did poor little Chloe—you did, darling, didn't you? You made every effort to be friends, wanted her so much to be your new sister! But, well...I do not wish to speak ill of Ellen, but nothing— absolutely nothing that we did—could please her. She was, I fear, set on resenting us. It upset her father dreadfully. Too late, he realised how much he'd spoiled her, made her possessive and cling- ing. *He* could control her a little, though not a great deal, but now that he is gone...' A little sob escaped her. 'Well, she has become as you see her.'

'She never goes *anywhere*!' Chloe exclaimed. 'She just buries herself here all year round.'

Pauline nodded. 'Sadly, that is true. She has her little teaching job at her old school—which in itself surely cannot be advisable, for it keeps her horizons from widening—but that is all she has. She has no social life—she rejects all my at- tempts to...to involve her!' She levelled her eyes at Max. 'I want nothing but the best for her. If Haughton holds too many memories for *me* to bear, for her I am sure it is much, much worse.

Doting on her father as she did was not emotionally healthy for a young woman...'

Max frowned. 'Did she not want her father to include you in his will? Neither you nor her stepsister?' he asked.

Was that the root of the matter? That Ellen Mountford had wanted everything her father had left to go to *her*, cutting out his second wife and stepdaughter completely?

'That may be so, alas,' confirmed Pauline. 'My poor Edward quite thought of Chloe as his own daughter—she took his name, as you know. Perhaps that led to some...well, perhaps some jealousy on Ellen's part? Possessive as she was about her father...'

Memory stung in Max's head. His mother might have taken his stepfather's name, but he— the nameless, fatherless bastard she had borne— had never been permitted to.

Pauline was speaking again, and he drew his mind back to the present.

'You must not think, Mr Vasilikos, that Edward has been in any way unfair to Ellen. Oh, he might have taken steps to ensure that Chloe and myself were taken care of financially, by way of including us in the ownership of this house, but Ellen was left everything else. And my husband…' she gave a sigh '…was a very wealthy man, with a substantial stock portfolio and other assets.' She took a little breath. 'Our share of this house, Mr Vasilikos, is all we have, Chloe and I, so I'm sure you will understand why, as well as finding being here without Edward too painful, we must sell. And,' she pointed out, 'of course Ellen's share of the sale price will be handsome.'

Max absorbed the information, keeping his expression impassive. What Pauline Mountford said rang all too true. That open bristling that he had seen from Ellen Mountford in her stepmother's company—

He got to his feet. There was nothing more to be achieved here right now. 'Well, I will leave it with you. See what you can do to change Ellen's mind and attitude.'

He smiled down at them—the courteous, impersonal smile he used to keep others well-disposed towards him for his own benefit.

Ten minutes later he was heading off down the drive, his glance going to either side, taking in one last sweep of the place. For now. His expression tightened. Whatever was necessary to induce Ellen Mountford to abandon her objection to selling her share of this place would, he determined as he turned out through the drawn-back iron gates on to the road, be done.

With or without her co-operation.

CHAPTER FOUR

MAX HEARD OUT his legal advisor, then drummed his fingers on the polished surface of his mahogany desk. Forcing a sale would indeed be time-consuming, and he wanted to take possession without delay—before summer was over. Which meant getting Ellen Mountford to drop her objections.

He gave a rasp of exasperation, swivelling moodily in his leather chair, his dark eyes baleful. There had been no good news from Pauline Mountford, and he strongly suspected there would not be. If Ellen was as entrenched in her hostile view of her stepmother as she seemed to be, then Pauline was doubtless the last person capable of changing her stepdaughter's mind.

But *he* might be able to.

An idea was forming in his head—he could feel it. An idea to make her *want* to sell up.

Chloe Mountford's voice echoed in his memory. *'She never goes anywhere—she just buries herself here all year round!'*

His eyes glinted. Maybe that was the key that would start to unlock the problem.

Impulsively he summoned his PA. 'Tell me, have I got any particularly glitzy social events coming up soon here in London?' he asked her.

Five minutes later he had his answer—and had made his decision. He sat back in his chair, long legs extended, a smile of satisfaction playing around his mouth. Oh, yes, he'd made his decision, all right. And Ellen herself had given him the way to convince her of it.

That mention she'd made of her surprising involvement in a charity for giving city children a countryside holiday under canvas. That would do nicely. Very nicely. His plan would help him lever Ellen Mountford out of his way—he was sure of it.

And as he settled down to work again, in a much better frame of mind, he became aware that he was sure of something else as well. That, of all things, he was looking forward to seeing her again—and making an end, once and for all, to all that nonsense of hers about looking the unappealing way she did.

I've seen her real body—her goddess body!—and now I want to see her face look just as good as her figure.

The smile played around his mouth once more, and the gleam in his eyes was speculative. Anticipatory.

And for a moment—just a moment—the prospect of finding a way to remove Ellen Mountford's objections to selling him the house he wanted to buy was not uppermost in his mind.

How good could she look? How good could she really look?

The glint came into his eye again. He wanted to find out.

Ellen turned off the ignition and got out. Her car needed a service, but she couldn't afford it. Her salary was wiped out simply paying for the essentials at Haughton—from council tax to electricity bills—and, of course, for the *in*essentials. Such as the weekly deliveries of hothouse flowers from the local florist, and Pauline and Chloe's regular visits to the local county town for their endless hair and beauty appointments. Their other extravagances—replenishing their wardrobes, their lavish social life and their foreign jaunts to luxury destinations and five-star hotels—were all funded by the stripping out of anything of value still left in the house, from paintings to *objets d'art.*

She hefted out a pile of schoolbooks, becoming aware of the sound of a vehicle approaching along the drive. As the sleek, powerful car turned into the courtyard dismay flooded through her. She'd hoped so much that Max Vasilikos had decided to buy somewhere else and abandoned his attentions to Haughton. Pauline and Chloe had finally lapsed into giving her the silent treatment, after having harangued her repeatedly about her stubbornness in refusing to do what they wanted her to do. Now they had taken themselves off again on yet another pricey jaunt, to a five-star hotel in Marbella while Ellen was just about to begin her school holidays.

Their departure had given Ellen cause for hope that Max Vasilikos had withdrawn his offer—in vain, it seemed. She watched him approach with a sinking heart—and also a quite different reaction that she tried to quash and failed utterly to do so. She gulped silently as he walked up to her, his handmade suit sheathing his powerful frame like a smooth, sleek glove. The dark eyes in his strong-featured face were levelled down at her. She felt her pulse leap.

It's just because I don't want him here. I don't want him going on at me to sell Haughton to him!

That was the reason for the sudden quickening of her breathing—the *only* reason she told herself urgently. The only reason she would allow... could possibly allow—

'Good afternoon, Miss Mountford,' he said. His voice was deep, and there was a hint of a curve at the corner of his sculpted mouth.

'What are you doing back here again?' she demanded. It was safer to sound antagonistic. Much safer.

Safer than standing here gazing gormlessly at him in all his incredible masculinity and gorgeousness. Feeling my heart thumping like an idiot and going red as a beetroot again!

Her hostile demand met with no bristling. Just the opposite. 'I wanted to see the rhododendrons,' Max returned blandly. 'They are indeed magnificent.' He paused, smiling his courteous social smile. 'Aren't you going to invite me in?' he said.

She glowered at him from behind her spectacles, her thick eyebrows forming that monobrow as she did so, and she was once again, he noted with displeasure, wearing the unspeakable baggy tracksuit that totally concealed her glorious body. Mentally, he earmarked it for the bonfire.

'Would it stop you if I didn't?' she glowered again.

'I doubt it,' he said, and then reached forward to remove half of the tottering tower of schoolbooks from her arms. 'After you,' he said, nodding at the kitchen door.

She cast him a burning look, refusing to say thank you for relieving her of much of her burden, and stomped indoors, dumping her load on the kitchen table. He deposited his share next to it.

'I hope you don't have to get all these marked for tomorrow,' he observed.

She shook her head. 'By the start of next term,' she said shortly.

'You've broken up?' enquired Max in a conversational tone. He knew perfectly well she had, as he'd had her term dates checked, and had timed his visit here accordingly.

'Today,' she said. She looked across at him. He seemed taller than ever in the kitchen, large though the space was. But then, she knew a man like Max Vasilikos could effortlessly dominate any space he occupied. 'You've wasted your journey,' she said bluntly. 'Pauline and Chloe left for Marbella yesterday.'

'Did they?' he returned carelessly. 'I'm not here to see them.'

Ellen lifted her eyes to him, glaring. 'Mr Vasilikos, *please* don't go on at me any more! Can't you just accept I don't want to sell Haughton?'

'I'm not here to talk about Haughton. I'm here to help your charity.'

Astonishment showed in her face and he went on smoothly.

'I'm confident I can increase your funding, enabling you to run camps more frequently. A national children's charity I support—for advantageous tax reasons—takes on new projects regularly. Yours I'm sure would be ideal for it.'

She was staring at him with an expression of extreme suspicion. 'Why would you do that?'

she demanded. 'Do you think it will change my mind about not selling Haughton?'

'Of course not,' he returned equably. 'My only concern is the deprived children. Is that not yours, too?' he countered, with precise gentleness and a bland look in his eye.

She took a breath. 'Well, if you can get us more funding we won't say no,' she managed to get out. There was something about the way he was casting a long look at her that threatened to bring the colour rushing to her cheeks.

'Good,' Max said. Then blithely went on. 'The thing is, though, you'll need to come up to London with me today—make a personal presentation. Time is very short—they have to spend the last of this year's money before the end of the financial year coming up.'

He was hustling her, he knew, and it was deliberate—he wanted to give her no excuse to get out of this.

'What?' Consternation filled Ellen's voice. 'Impossible!'

'No, it's quite all right—it won't inconvenience me at all,' said Max in a smooth voice, deliberately misunderstanding the cause of her objection. He glanced at his watch. 'You go off and get ready while I take another stroll around the gardens—admire those rhododendrons!' He smiled at her, completely ignoring the fact that her mouth was opening to object yet again. 'I'll give you twenty minutes,' he said blandly, and was gone.

Ellen stared after him, open-mouthed. Consternation was tumbling around inside her—shot through with aftershock. Slowly she gathered her composure back, by dint of piling her marking neatly into class rows. Did Max Vasilikos *really* imagine she'd waltz off with him to London for the day, to pitch for more funding for her camping project?

More money would be really helpful right now. We could double the numbers at the half-term session—buy more tents and sleeping bags. Run another week in the summer holidays...

The problem was, though, she thought, as she descended to earth with a bump, that in order to get her hands on the funding she'd have to sit next to Max Vasilikos all the way to London, enclosed in his car. Would she be a captive audience for his determination to wrest Haughton from her?

But the reverse will be true, too. If he goes on at me, then he'll also have to listen to me telling him I'm never going to agree to sell. Never!

Yes, that was the way to think—and *not* about the way the image of Max Vasilikos, seen again now in all its devastating reality, was busy burning itself into her retinas and making her heart beat faster. Because what possible point was there in her pulse quickening? If even ordinary men looked right past her, wanting only to look at Chloe, then to a man like Max Vasilikos, who romanced film stars, she must be completely invisible.

In a way, that actually made it easier. Easier for her to change into something more suitable for London—the well-worn dark grey suit and white blouse that she donned for parents' evenings and school functions, and sturdy, comfortable lace-ups, before confining her unruly hair into a lumpy bun—and then heading back out into the courtyard.

Max Vasilikos was already behind the wheel of his monstrous beast of a car, and he leant across to open the passenger door. She got into the low-slung seat awkwardly, feeling suddenly that despite being invisible to him, as she knew she was, *he* was very, very visible to her.

And very close.

With a shake of her head, to clear her stupid thoughts, she fastened her seat belt as he set off with a throaty growl of the engine. Oh, Lord, was she insane to head off with him like this? All the way to London in the all too close confines of his car? She sat back tensely, fingers clutching the handbag in her lap.

'So, tell me more about this charity of yours,' Max invited as he turned out of the drive on to the narrow country lane beyond. He wanted to set her at ease, not have her sitting there tense as a board.

Gratefully Ellen answered, explaining how she and a fellow teacher had started it two years ago. She also told him about their hopes for expansion, which more funding would definitely enable.

Max continued to ask questions that drew her out more, and as she talked he could see she was gradually starting to relax. The enthusiasm he'd seen so briefly over lunch the other day was coming through again, and she was becoming animated as she spoke. He moved the subject on from the practicalities of the venture to some of its underlying issues.

'How do you find the children respond to the camping?' he asked.

'Usually very well,' she replied. 'They all have to do chores, share the work, and most discover grit and strength in themselves—a determination to achieve goals that will, we hope, enable them to transfer those lessons to their future and make something of themselves, despite their disadvantaged and often troubled backgrounds.'

She became aware that Max was looking at her, a revealing expression on his face.

'Reminds me of myself,' he said. 'When my mother died I had to make my own way in the world—and it definitely took grit and strength and determination. Starting with nothing and building myself up from scratch.'

She glanced at him curiously. 'You weren't born to all this, then?' she asked, indicating the luxury car they were sitting in.

He gave a short, humourless laugh. 'I worked five years on building sites to make enough to buy a ruin that I then spent two years restoring myself and selling on. I took the profit to do the same again and again, until I'd bootstrapped my way up to where I am now,' he told her. His sideways glance was caustic, but there was a trace of mordant humour in it. 'Does that improve your opinion of me at all?' he posed.

She swallowed. She would have to give him his due—anything else would be unfair, however unwelcome he was in her life. 'I respect you for all the hard work you've obviously had to put in to make yourself rich. My only objection to you, Mr Vasilikos, is that you want to buy Haughton and I don't want to sell it to you.'

Belatedly she realised that she herself had brought the subject back to what she did *not* want to discuss—selling her home. But to her relief he did not respond in kind.

'Tell me, how old were you when your mother died?' he asked instead.

Her eyes widened and she stared at him, wondering why he was asking such a personal, intrusive question. Then something he'd said chimed in her head. *'When my mother died...'*

'Fifteen,' she answered. 'She was killed in a head-on car crash.'

'I was the same age when mine died,' Max said.

His voice was neutral, but it did not deceive Ellen.

'She died of lung disease.' There was a slight pause. 'It's not a good age to lose a parent,' he said.

'When *is*?' returned Ellen quietly. It was strange to think of this man, from so utterly different a world from her, having that same tragedy in her life as she did. To think that they, who were so utterly, glaringly unalike, had that in common.

'Indeed.'

He was silent a moment, manoeuvring the car effortlessly around a tight bend, accelerating out of it. When he spoke again it was to return to the subject of the charity and what financial constraints further funding might alleviate.

Ellen was relieved—talking about such deeply felt emotional issues with this man was...*strange*. Yet even though he'd changed the subject, reverted to his smooth, urbane social manner, she felt a curious sense of having somehow touched a chord in him, drawn by the mutual personal tragedy in their lives.

They joined the motorway soon after, and Max

could let the car really rip, cruising down the fast lane as if merely out for a stroll. His mind cruised too. Ellen Mountford was definitely losing that excruciating self-consciousness that had dominated her reaction to him up till now, and he was glad of it. It helped that they could talk without looking at each other, and that he had the road to focus on. It seemed to take some of the pressure off her. But there was more to it than that, he was aware. That oh-so-brief mention of his mother—and hers—had been like a flicker of real communication between them. Something that could not have happened between two mere social acquaintances.

He frowned. *Do I want that? Do I want any real communication with her? Why should I? She is merely someone standing in the way of what I am determined to achieve—ownership of a house I want to live in myself. And bringing her up to London is merely the means to that end. Nothing more than that.*

His expression lightened. Of course there was one other reason for bringing Ellen Mountford to London with him. He was all too conscious of that too.

I want to see what she can really look like— when she makes the most of herself instead of the least!

And he would want to know that, he realised, even if she'd had absolutely nothing to do with blocking his way to the house he wanted to possess. Curiosity was mounting within him about Ellen Mountford for herself—not for her house. Across his retinas flickered the recalled image of her in her running gear, showing off that fantastic figure. Which was more than could be said for what she was wearing now—it was no better than the tracksuit. A heavy, badly cut suit and the same ill-fitting white blouse, and those ugly lace-up shoes, which were doing absolutely nothing for her.

A smile flickered about his mouth. What he had in mind for her to wear tonight was quite different...

He dragged his thoughts away and went back into making easy-going conversation with her, taking the opportunity of their passing Windsor Castle to ask something about the British Royal Family. She answered readily enough, and he asked another question to keep her talking.

It dawned on him that she wasn't actually shy at all. Away from her stepmother and stepsister she was noticeably more voluble. Animation lifted her features, lighting up her tawny eyes even behind the concealing lenses of her unflattering glasses, and helping to detract from that damn monobrow of hers which made her look as if she was always frowning. Now that he was seeing her again, he realised, it was clear that actually she didn't look nearly as morosely forbidding as she had when in the company of her stepmother and sister.

So, if she wasn't shy, why the total lack of personal grooming? Why look as dire as she did, considering that she could look so much better?

The question circled in his head as they approached London and headed for the West End, eventually drawing up at his hotel in Piccadilly. His passenger looked at him in surprise.

'I thought we were going to the charity's headquarters,' she said, 'so I can make my pitch for funding?'

Max smiled at her. 'Not exactly,' he said, getting out of the car.

A doorman was opening her door, and as she

got out, seeing Max toss the keys to the valet parker, Ellen was suddenly conscious of her plain, dowdy appearance. Utterly unworthy of such a smart hotel—or for keeping company with a man like Max.

'This way,' he said blandly, ushering her inside and guiding her across the swish lobby towards a bank of lifts.

They whooshed upwards, and when they emerged she saw with a frown that they were on the penthouse floor and Max was leading her into one of the suites. She gazed around, confused, taking in the lavish decor of a vast lounge and huge windows overlooking St James's Park. Max was speaking.

'I have not been entirely comprehensive in what I've told you,' he said, his voice bland. He quirked one eyebrow. 'You don't make your pitch now—you make it tonight.' His smile deepened. 'At the ball.'

Ellen stared. 'Ball?' she echoed blankly.

'Yes,' said Max, in that same smooth, urbane manner. 'The annual fundraising ball the charity always holds at this hotel. You'll be sitting on my table, and so will one of the charity's directors. You can have a little chat then, tell him about the camping holidays and what funds you need to expand them.'

Ellen felt the floor disappear from under her. 'I *cannot* go to a *ball*!' she said. The man was mad—completely mad!

'Ah, well,' said Max, his voice as smooth as cream, his smile as rich as butter, 'in that I have to say you are quite, quite mistaken.'

CHAPTER FIVE

ELLEN TOOK A BREATH. Or tried to. There didn't seem to be any breath left in her body because her lungs seemed to be caught in a vice. Horror drenched her—horror at the very thought of being paraded at a *ball* with Max Vasilikos. Her mortification would be exquisite, unbearable—hideous! As hideous as her appearance would be. She felt the colour drain from her cheeks and there was a sick feeling in her stomach.

Max was continuing to speak, still in that same blandly smooth way. 'If you're worried because you have nothing to wear, don't be. I'll have some suitable gowns delivered and you can make your choice. We'll have lunch first, and then afterwards I'll leave you in the hands of the stylists I've booked—it's all arranged. Now...' His tone changed and he walked to the house phone on the desk at the side of the room. 'Time for that lunch. Would you like a preprandial drink? You look somewhat pale.'

In fact she looked like a dish of curds and whey, he decided, and without waiting for an answer crossed to the drinks cabinet and found a bottle of sherry, pouring her a generous measure.

'Drink up,' he said cheerfully.

She took it with nerveless fingers but did not drink. Instead she made her voice work, though it sounded like creaky hinges. 'Mr Vasilikos, I cannot possibly go through with this! It's very... kind...' she almost choked on the word '...of you, but...but...no, I can't. It's out of the question. Impossible. Unthinkable.' She swallowed. Made herself look at him. 'Unthinkable,' she said again, trying desperately to put a note of finality into her strangled voice.

It did not work. He simply gave her a straight look. She'd reverted, he could see, to having that grim expression on her face she'd had when he'd gone to Haughton to view it. It didn't suit her—beetling her monobrow and pulling heavily at her features.

'Why?' He gave her an encouraging smile. 'You'll enjoy it, I promise you.'

She swallowed again. 'I'm *not*, Mr Vasilikos, a party animal.' There was strain in her voice, as if she were forcing herself to speak. 'I think that's pretty obvious.'

He was undeterred. 'It will do you good,' he said blandly.

A knock on the door diverted him and he went to open it. Lunch had arrived.

'Come and sit down,' invited Max, and gestured to the table once all the food had been laid out for them and the servers had departed.

Involuntarily, Ellen felt hungry suddenly. She also realised she must have gulped down half the sherry, for there was a taste of alcohol in her throat. She'd better eat something now...

I'll eat lunch, then head off to the station and get home. Maybe if I write to the charity director he'll consider my application anyway.

Because doing what Max was so ludicrously suggesting was out of the question—just totally out of the question.

Thank God he hadn't mentioned me going to the ball in front of Chloe. She'd have had a field day, sneering and mocking me. Laughing like a hyena at the thought of me dressed up for an evening with Max Vasilikos!

Cold snaked down her spine as she made a start on her meal. It was delicious, she noticed absently—a seafood terrine with a saffron sauce, and keeping warm an entrée of lamb fillet. Hunger spiked in her and she tucked in. From the other end of the table Max glanced at her. It was good, he realised, to see a woman eating well. Not that it would put any fat on her—he knew that now. Not with a toned, sleek body like hers. Memory leapt in his head at just how toned and sleek her body was, and how it was that he'd discovered the amazing truth about this woman he'd crassly assumed was overweight.

'Did you go running this morning?' he heard himself enquire.

She looked up. 'I run every morning,' she said. 'Plus I use the school gym and the pool. Taking Games lessons also keeps me pretty active.'

'Hockey?' Max asked interestedly.

She shook her head. 'Lacrosse. A much better game!' There was a note of enthusiasm in her voice that even her dismay at Max Vasilikos's absurd notion of taking her to a ball—a *ball*, for heaven's sake!—could not squash.

Well, she wouldn't be going to any ball—with or without him, tonight or any other night—so there was no point worrying about it. She would just put it out of her head, enjoy this delicious lunch, and then head for the station. Maybe she'd look in at the Natural History Museum in South Kensington, get some more ideas for her Geography classes, pick up some learning material for her pupils. Yes, that was what she would do.

Relaxing slightly at the realisation that of *course* Max Vasilikos couldn't make her go to this ridiculous ball of his, she heard him asking, 'Isn't lacrosse somewhat violent?' He frowned.

She shook her head again. 'You're thinking of men's lacrosse. That can be vicious! But then so can men's hockey. Girls play a gentler game. But it's fast and furious for all that. I've always loved it. Nothing to beat it.' There was open enthusiasm in her voice now.

'Were you in the team when you were at school?' Max asked.

It was good to hear her speak without that note of almost panic in her voice that had been there as she'd reacted to his mention of the evening's ball, and he knew it was necessary for him to back off for a while, let her calm down again. Her forbidding expression was ebbing, too, and that *had* to be good.

Besides, it was, he realised, something of a pleasant novelty to be lunching with a female in his private suite and not have her endlessly making doe eyes at him, batting her eyelashes, trying to flirt and get his attention. With Ellen there was no such tedious predictability. Instead it was refreshing to talk to a woman about keeping fit, exercise and sport—all of which he enjoyed robustly himself. And she was clearly in her element on such subjects, knowledgeable and confident.

She nodded, then answered him. 'On the wing—loads of running there.'

He glanced at her speculatively. 'What about Chloe? Was she sporty?'

He knew perfectly well she wouldn't have been, but he wanted to hear what Ellen would say about the stepsister she so glaringly resented. Would she despise her for not being in the team?

A tight look had formed in Ellen's eyes. 'Chloe wasn't in the sporty crowd,' she said.

Max picked his next words with deliberate care. 'It must have been difficult for her, joining a new school after her mother married your father. She must have looked to you to help her fit in.'

Ellen's expression froze. Memory pushed into her head. Vivid and painful.

Chloe, with her long blonde tresses, her supercilious air of sophistication and her worldly experience of boys and smoking and alcohol and fashion and music and make-up, had been instantly accepted into a bitchy, cliquey set of girls just like her, effortlessly becoming the meanest of the mean girls, sneering at everyone else. Sneering most of all at her hulking, clumping, games-loving stepsister, who'd so stupidly tried to befriend her initially, when she'd actually believed that her father's remarriage might bring him happiness instead of misery and ruin.

Max's eyes rested on Ellen, seeing her expression close up. Had he hit home? he wondered. He hoped so—because it was for her own good, after all, getting her to face up to what was keeping her trapped in the bitter, resentful, narrow life she led, refusing to move on from the past.

She has to let go of her resentment against her stepfamily, stop using her share of their inheritance as a weapon against them. Stop clinging to the past instead of moving into the future. I need to bring her out of herself. Show her the world beyond the narrow confines she's locked herself into—let her embrace it...enjoy it.

And what could be more enjoyable than a ball? A glittering, lavish affair that she might enjoy if only she would give herself a chance to do so! But for now he would not press her. For now he just wanted to keep her in this unselfconscious, relaxed zone. So he didn't wait for an answer to his pointed comment about Chloe, but turned the subject back to an easier topic that she clearly found less uncomfortable.

'What kind of workout routine do you do?' he asked. 'You must use weights, I take it?'

To his surprise she flushed that unflattering red that he'd seen all too frequently on his first visit to Haughton.

'That's pretty obvious, isn't it?' she mumbled, knowing he'd have spotted her developed muscle tone—so mercilessly mocked by Chloe, who jibed at her for being more like a man than a woman—when he'd seen her in running gear. 'But I'm good at them and I enjoy it.'

Was there a defensive note to her voice—defiance, even? If so, Max wondered why. She obviously had a fantastic physique—he'd seen that for himself, and had very much enjoyed doing so! But she was speaking again now, and he drew his mind back from that tantalising vision of her fabulous body when she'd been out running.

'I balance weights with cardio work, obviously, but I'd rather run than cycle. Especially since it's such a joy to run in the grounds at home—' She broke off, a shadow in her eyes. Those glorious early-morning runs she loved to take would become a thing of the past if Haughton were wrenched from her...

'What about rowing?' Max asked, cutting across her anguished thoughts. 'That's a good combo of cardio and strength work. It's my favourite, I admit. Though only on a machine.' He gave a rueful smile. 'When I'm on the water I'd rather swim, sail or windsurf.'

She made herself smile. 'Well, you've got the

weather for that in Greece!' she riposted lightly, glad to be away from the subject of her overdeveloped muscles, which so embarrassed her. She knew she was being stupid, feeling self-conscious about it with a man who couldn't care less what she looked like as a woman. Inevitably she was invisible to him in that respect. Much less stressful to blank all that and just talk to him as she'd been doing, about sport and exercise, without any connotations about the impact on her appearance.

'It must be great not to need a wetsuit,' she said enviously.

'Agreed.' Max smiled, glad that he was getting her to relax again.

Deliberately he kept the conversation going along convivial lines, asking her about her experiences in water sport, which seemed to be mainly focussed on school trips to the Solent—definitely wetsuits required. Equally deliberately he waxed lyrical about how enjoyable it was to pursue water sports in warmer climes, recommending several spots he knew well. He wanted to open her mind to the possibilities of enjoying the wider world—once she had freed herself from the self-inflicted confines of her past, stopped clinging to the house he wanted her to let go of.

But with the arrival of the dessert course he steered the conversation back to the reason for her presence here.

As they helped themselves to *tarte au citron* Max was pleased to see Ellen tucking in with obvious enjoyment. *It's a sensual pleasure, enjoying food.* The thought was in his head before he could stop it. And the corollary that went with it. *There are more sensual pleasures than food for her to enjoy...*

The words hovered in his head, but he put them firmly aside. They were inappropriate. All he was doing was introducing her to the delights that could be hers if she embraced the world instead of hiding away from it.

Starting tonight.

He pushed his empty plate away and glanced at his watch. 'We've time for coffee, then a team of stylists are arriving and I'll leave you to them.' He smiled at Ellen.

Her fork promptly clattered to the plate. She was looking at him, her former ease vanished, her expression now one of panic. Panic that changed to a kind of gritty stoniness. He'd seen that look before, and knew it meant she was locking herself down into herself again.

She began to speak, her voice as tight as her expression as she bit the words out. 'Mr Vasilikos—look, I'm sure you mean well, in your own way, but I really, *really* don't want to go to this ball tonight! It would be...' she swallowed '...horrendous.'

He levelled his gaze at her. 'Why?' he demanded simply.

Ellen felt her hands clench the edge of the table as if it might support her. Then she forced herself to speak. To spell out the brutal truth he seemed oblivious to for reasons she could not fathom. She had to disabuse him of *any* notion that going to a ball would be anything other than unspeakable torment for her.

'Because,' she said, and it dawned on him that she was speaking as if she were talking to a particularly intellectually challenged pupil, 'you said it to me yourself at Haughton, when you saw me running. You said, *"You're nothing like your stepsister Chloe."* You couldn't have made it plainer. And you're absolutely right—I *am* nothing at all like Chloe and I never have been. I accept that completely—I've no illusions about myself, believe me. I know exactly what I look like. *That* is why going to a ball, or anything resembling a ball, or any social gathering of any kind at all is anathema to me. The very thought of dressing up and trying to be…trying to be…trying to be *anything* like Chloe—'

There was a choking sound in her voice and she broke off. She felt as if the blood was curdling in her veins—as if Chloe herself were standing there, her mocking peal of derisive laughter lashing at her at the very *thought* of her going to a ball—and with Max Vasilikos of all men! Her eyes tightened shut again, screwing up in their sockets, and her fingers indented into the wood of the table as she gripped it. Then her eyes flew open again.

'I *know* what I am. What I've always been. What I always will be. I'm pushing six foot tall, I've got size eight feet and I've got muscles that can bench fifty kilos. I'm like some *gigantic elephant* compared with Chloe.'

The misery and the self-loathing in her face was contorting her features. Consuming her.

Across the table Max had sat back, gazing at her with a new expression on his face. Abruptly he spoke.

'Tell me, do you think Chloe beautiful?' There was a strange note in his voice. Enlightenment was dawning in him like a tsunami in slow motion. Was *this* what was screwing up Ellen Mountford?

Ellen stared. 'What kind of question is that? Of *course* she is! She's everything I'm not. She's petite and incredibly slim, and she has a heart-shaped face and blue eyes and blonde hair.'

The new expression on Max's face did not change. 'And if I described her,' he said carefully, his eyes not letting her go for an instant, 'as… let's see…like a scrawny chicken, what would you say?' Deliberately he chose as harsh a term as she had used about herself to make his point.

She said nothing. Only stared at him, not un-derstanding. Incapable of understanding, Max realised with dawning comprehension. He shook his head slightly. 'You wouldn't believe me, would you?' His voice changed, becoming in-cisive, incontrovertible. 'Do you not realise,' he demanded, 'that it is only *you* who thinks you are like an elephant?'

She stared at him. Her face was expressionless. Her voice as she answered him toneless. 'Chloe thinks so too.'

She revels in thinking it. Taunts me endlessly. Is viciously gleeful about it. Goes on and on about it! Has tortured me ever since she and her vulture of a mother smashed my life to pieces—going on and on at me about how big I am, how heavy I am, how clumping and lumping and pathetically, pitifully plain and repulsive I am, how I'm just an embarrassing joke! Someone to laugh at and sneer at and look down on! Elephant Ellen...

Max made a sound in his throat and his dark eyes flashed. 'And has it never dawned on you that Chloe, with her tiny size zero frame, would consider a greyhound to be the size of an elephant?' He took a heavy breath and his eyes bored into her. Something in Greek escaped his lips.

Ellen could only stare at him, her face stricken at the ugly memory of Chloe's years of merciless cruelty about her appearance.

'I fully appreciate,' he said, now speaking in

English, spelling out each word carefully, emphatically, so that they would penetrate her skull, reach deep inside her where they needed to reach, 'that for whatever reason—the fashion industry, the prevalence of eating disorders and God knows what else!—extreme thinness is currently regarded as beautiful. And I fully appreciate,' he went on, not letting Ellen do anything except sit and stare at him with blank eyes full of helpless misery, 'that Chloe happens to fit the current description of what makes for a "fashionable" figure. But—'

He held his hand up now, silencing any retort she might have been likely to make.

'That is entirely and completely irrelevant. Because *you*, Ellen…' He paused, and a new timbre suddenly underlaid his voice, resonating through words that echoed in the sudden shift in his expression. 'You,' he breathed, and his eyes were boring into hers, never letting them go for an instant, an iota, 'have the body of a goddess. A *goddess*, Ellen.'

There was silence—complete silence. Max let his eyes rest on her, saying nothing more. Watching her react. It was like a slow-motion sequence in a movie. Red washed into her face like a tide, then drained out, leaving it white and stark. Her eyes distended, then shut like the shell of a clam.

'Don't,' she said. 'Please don't.'

But he did. 'The body of a goddess,' he repeated. 'Don't tell me you don't—because I've seen it. I've seen damn nearly all of it. And believe me...'

Suddenly his long, long lashes swept down over his dark, dark eyes and Ellen felt a kind of hollowing out in her stomach that had nothing to do with the tide of misery that had been drowning her and everything to do with the hot, humid memory of how she'd been wearing only a sports bra and brief shorts when he'd seen her out running that time.

'I liked what I saw. I liked it, Ellen...' and now there was a huskiness in his voice '...a lot.'

He shifted in his seat, relaxing now, his broad shoulders moulding the back of the chair, a smile starting to curve his mouth. 'I've seen a lot of women with fantastic figures, Ellen—and my time with Tyla Brentley, especially when I was out in LA with her, supplied that amply!—so

I promise you, you can trust my judgement on these matters. And you can trust my word, too.'

His expression changed, and so did his voice.

'My word,' he announced, 'is that I will donate five thousand pounds to your city kids charity today if you will agree to the following. To put yourself into the hands of the team of stylists this afternoon and let them do whatever it is they do. When they've done it, if you still don't want to come to the ball tonight I will let you off and double the five thousand pounds. If you *do* want to come, however, I'll triple it.' He gave a brief, slashing smile. 'Deal?' he posed.

Ellen stared back.

Five thousand pounds… Ten—because of course it *would* be ten! Of course she wouldn't want to go to the ball tonight. No way on God's earth would she volunteer for such an ordeal, however desperately she was scrubbed at by whatever professional make-up artists and the like he had lined up. Yet even as she made that mental averment she could still hear his voice echoing in her head.

The body of a goddess, Ellen.

She heard it, felt it—felt its power. Its temptation.

'Well?' he prompted.

He was holding his hand out across the table. His large, square, strong hand. Into which slowly—very slowly—her own hand seemed to be placing itself, though her head was still reeling with what he'd said to her.

'Good,' said Max. 'So that's all settled, then.' Satisfaction was blatant in his voice. He sat back, withdrawing his hand, moving it towards the coffee pot and starting to pour. 'Cream?' he asked, with a lift of his eyebrow, and poured it in anyway. With a honed, toned body like hers she could drink cream by the bucketload and it would never turn to fat.

Goddess body sorted. Now all that was needed was to sort out the rest of her appearance. Happy anticipation filled him.

People were doing things to Ellen. She had no idea what, and she didn't care. Even about the painful bits that involved tweezers and razors, hot wax and skin peels. She shut her eyes mostly, and let them get on with it, focussing her mind on what she'd do with the ten thousand pounds she'd get for the charity when they'd finished with her.

There were three of them working on her, stylists, beauticians, hairdressers. Whatever they were, they were chattering away. They were all stick-thin, just like Chloe, all wearing ultra-fashionable clothes and four-inch heels, with sharp hairstyles and loads of make-up—which was par for the course, Ellen reasoned, if one worked in the beauty industry. Their conversation seemed to be about clubs and bands, film stars and fashion brands, about which they were intimately knowledgeable.

They looked about twenty and made her feel like thirty. She hoped they were getting paid generously by Max, considering the impossibility of what they were attempting—making her look good enough to go to a ball. Because of course that was impossible. How could it be otherwise?

Dear God, how Chloe would laugh like a hyena if she could see this. She'd be filming it on her phone, posting it to her bitchy friends on social media, and they'd be squealing with laughter. Elephant Ellen, trying to look glamorous! How hilarious! How beyond pathetic!

Cold ran through her at the thought. Well, she'd be spared Chloe's mockery. Because the moment she had that cheque for ten thousand pounds in her hands she'd wipe off all the gunk the stylists were putting on her, get back into her school suit and head home. Back to the safety of Haughton—blessedly hers alone for the next few weeks while Pauline and Chloe were away. Hers to make the most of…the very, very most…

While she could.

Fear bit at her. Max Vasilikos was powerful, rich and ruthless. He'd clearly set his mind on trying to eject her, and he probably had the financial means to do so. It would cost him—but did he care? Maybe he was one of those men who had to win at any price. Wasn't what he was attempting this evening proof of it? Resorting to trying to flatter her into submission?

Telling me I have the body of a goddess!

She heard his voice again in her head, low and husky.

She silenced it.

She realised that one of the stylists, who was busy painting her nails a dark crimson—or the nail extensions that had been stuck on—was talking to her.

'You are *so* lucky to be going out with Max

Vasilikos tonight.' There was open envy in her voice. 'He's just to die for!'

Mortified, Ellen steeled her jaw. 'This isn't a *date*,' she said, horrified at the implication and trying desperately to sound composed. 'It's a charity fundraiser.'

Her protestation was ignored. 'He took Tyla Brentley last year,' the second stylist confirmed, doing something with long pins and a curling tong to Ellen's newly cut, coloured and piled up hair. 'She was a sensation.'

'Her dress was stunning' said the third, applying yet more mascara to Ellen's eyelashes, having already lavished eyeshadow and eyeliner plentifully upon her.

'It was Verensiana, and the shoes were Senda Sorn,' the first rattled off knowledgeably. 'She wore Verensiana to the film awards this year too—he's her *totes* fave designer. She went with Ryan Rendell, of course—they are *so* an item now!' She sighed soulfully, and then her eyes brightened as she smiled encouragingly at Ellen. 'Don't worry—she is, like, so *totally* over Max Vasilikos now. So the coast is completely clear for you.'

Ellen let them babble on, not bothering to try and refute their insanely wrong assumptions. Nails finished, the stylist dried them off with a hairdryer, before standing back with the other two stylists, who'd also finished whatever it was they'd been doing to her.

'OK,' announced the first stylist, 'let's go for the gown!'

Resigned, Ellen got to her feet, as requested, shedding the cotton robe she'd been inserted into after bathing, standing there in underwear that consisted of a low-cut underwired bra that hoicked up her breasts, plus lacy panties and black stockings—a universe away from her usual plain and serviceable underwear. As for the gown that had been selected for her, she had no idea and didn't care. It wouldn't be on for long anyway—just long enough for her to tell Max to hand over the cheque for ten thousand pounds.

But as she watched one of the trio fetch the gown out of the wardrobe she gasped. 'What is *that*?' she breathed.

'Isn't it *fabulous*?' came the answer.

'But it's...it's...'

'Edwardian,' said one of the others confidently.

'You know—like Victorian, but later. But not flappers like the roaring twenties.' She looked at Ellen. 'Didn't you know it was a costume ball?'

No, Ellen had not known. Had not known anything of the sort.

And right now, as the trio started to help her step into the stiffly draped dark red skirts and draw up the whalebone bodice so that it fitted tightly over her bust, pulling narrow straps over her shoulders to flare outwards in a spray of black feathers, her only conscious thought was that it was going to be hellish getting herself out of the dress again when she changed back into her own clothes. There must be a zillion hooks to undo.

CHAPTER SIX

Max gave his bow tie a final twitch. Thank heavens Edwardian male evening dress was not a million miles from modern formal wear. It was very different for women. An anticipatory gleam lit his eye. Oh, he was looking forward to this. He was really, *really* looking forward to it. It would cost him fifteen thousand pounds, but it would be money well spent, he was sure—and not just for the sake of the charity!

Checking his cuffs, he strolled to the drinks cabinet, extracting a chilled bottle of vintage champagne and setting it down by two flutes. The noise at the bedroom door made him turn. It was not the stylists—they'd already gone in a flurry of chatter and on their phones already. Ellen was emerging.

His eyes narrowed. And then—

Yes! He wanted to punch the air in triumph. *Yes, yes, yes!*

He watched her walk into the room in a trail of long skirts. She halted abruptly when she saw him. He saw her face tighten.

'OK,' she said, 'where's this cheque you promised me?'

She spoke brusquely, because Max's eyes were like a hawk's on her, and it made her feel acutely, agonisingly uncomfortable. Even though she hadn't looked at her own reflection yet—she couldn't bear to!—she knew exactly what he was seeing. A big, hulking woman in a ridiculously tightly laced preposterous costume dress, with a tottering hairstyle and a face full of make-up that did absolutely nothing for her—because she had a face for which absolutely nothing could be done and that was all there was to it.

Yet again in her head she heard the peal of Chloe's derisive laughter mocking her...mocking the pathetic attempt to make Elephant Ellen look glamorous.

Well, she didn't care—*wouldn't* care. She only wanted the cheque that Max Vasilikos had promised her, then she was getting out of this ridiculous get-up—zillion hooks or not—and high-tailing it to the station and home.

Max smiled his urbane, social smile and reached inside his breast pocket. 'Here you go,' he said, and held the cheque he'd promised out to her.

Awkwardly, Ellen walked over and took it. Then her expression altered and her gaze snapped back to him. 'This is for *fifteen* thousand,' she objected.

'Of course it is,' he agreed affably. 'Because of course you're coming to the ball with me. We're both kitted up—let's have a look at ourselves. See if we look the part.'

He helped himself to her arm with a white-gloved hand—he was wearing evening dress of the same Edwardian era, she realised, but on a man it was a lot less immediately obvious—and turned her towards a huge framed mirror hung above a sideboard.

'Take a look, Ellen,' he instructed softly.

Ellen looked.

And made no response. Could have made no response even if someone had shouted *Fire!* Could only do what she was doing—which was staring. Staring, frozen, at the couple reflected in the mirror. At the tall, superbly elegant and dashing figure of Max Vasilikos—and the tall, superbly elegant and stunning woman at his side.

The dark ruby-red silk gown was wasp-waisted and moulded over her hips to flow in a waterfall of colour the full length of her legs and out into a sweeping train, the body-hugging boned bodice revealed a generous décolletage, and the spray of feathers at each sculpted shoulder matched the similar spray in the aigrette curving around the huge swirled pompadour of her hair.

Curling tendrils played around her face—a face whose eyes were huge beneath winged, arched brows...rich tawny eyes that were thickly lashed and fathoms deep—a face whose cheeks were sculpted as if from marble, whose mouth was as lush and richly hued as damsons.

'Didn't I tell you?' Max said softly to her, because he could see from the expression on her face that something profoundly important and significant was happening to her. She was seeing, for the first time in her life, someone she had never seen before—the strikingly, dramatically beautiful woman that was looking back at her from the glass. 'A goddess,' he murmured. 'Didn't I tell you? In figure and in face...like

Artemis the huntress goddess…strong and lithe and so, so beautiful.'

He let his gaze work over her reflection, drinking in face and figure, her beauty fully and finally revealed to him. A frown flickered in his eyes. 'Have you put in contact lenses?' he heard himself ask. What had happened to those wretched unflattering spectacles of hers?

She gave a slight shake of her head, feeling the soft tendrils curling down from her extravagant hairdo wafting softly and sensuously at her jaw.

'I only really need glasses for driving,' she answered. 'But I wear them because—' She stopped, swallowed.

Max said nothing—but he knew. Oh, he knew now why she wore them.

Ellen's eyes slid away. Her voice was heavy, and halting. 'I wear them to tell the world that I know perfectly well how awful I look, and that I accept it and I'm not going to make a pathetic fool of myself trying to look better, not going to try to—'

She broke off. Max finished the painful, self-condemning sentence for her.

'Not going to try to compete with your stepsister,' he said, his voice low.

Ellen nodded. 'Pathetic, I know. But—'

He caught her other arm, turning her to face him. '*No!* Don't think like that!' His expression was vehement, even fierce, as she stared at him. 'Ellen, whatever you've come to think in your head about yourself it's *wrong*!' He took a breath. 'Don't you realise you don't *have* to compete with Chloe? Leave her to enjoy her fashionable thinness! You...' His voice changed. 'Ah, *you* have a quite, quite different beauty.' He lifted a hand to gesture to her reflection. 'How can you possibly deny that now?'

Ellen gazed, her mind still trying to keep on denying what Max was saying to her—what the reflection in the mirror was telling her. That a stunningly beautiful woman was gazing back at her. A woman who was...*her*...

But that was impossible! It *had* to be impossible. It was *Chloe* who was lovely—*Chloe* who possessed the looks that defined beauty.

And if it was *Chloe* who was lovely, then she, Ellen, who was everything that Chloe was not—not petite, not blonde, not thin, not with a heart-shaped face, not blue-eyed, not *Chloe*—could only be the opposite. If it were *Chloe* who was lovely—then she, Ellen, could only be *un*lovely.

That was the logic that had been forced on her—forced on her with every sneering barb from Chloe, every derisive glance, every mocking jibe from her stepsister—for years... Those vulnerable teenage years when Chloe had arrived to poison her life, poison her mind against herself, destroying all her confidence so that she'd never even tried to make something of herself, instead condemning herself as harshly as her stepsister condemned her. Believing in Chloe's contempt of her. Seeing herself only through Chloe's cruel eyes.

But how could the woman gazing out at her from the mirror with such dramatic beauty possibly be described as unlovely? How could a woman like that be sneered at by Chloe, mocked by her, treated with contempt by her?

Impossible—just impossible. Impossible for Chloe to sneer at a woman such as the one who was gazing back at her now.

Emotion swept through Ellen. She couldn't give a name to it—didn't need to. Needed only to feel it rush through her like a tide, sweeping away everything that had been inside her head for so many years. And now Max was speaking again, adding to the tide sweeping through her.

'You can't deny it, can you?' Max repeated. His eyes were fixed on her reflection still. 'You can't deny your beauty—your own beauty, Ellen. *Yours.* As different from Chloe's as the sun is from the moon.'

He gave a laugh suddenly, of triumph and deep satisfaction.

'We shall drink a toast,' he announced. 'A toast to the goddess revealed.' He drew her away, towards the tray of champagne, opening the bottle with skilled long practice and filling the flutes to hand one to her.

Ellen took it numbly, her eyes wide, as if she was in a dream. A dream she still could not quite believe was reality after all.

Her eyes flickered back to her reflection in the mirror.

Is it really, truly me? Can it be—?

Then Max's gloved hand was touching her wrist, lifting his own foaming glass, and she looked back at him, still with that bemused expression in her eyes, as if she dared not believe the truth of her own reflection. He held her gaze, not letting go for an instant.

'To you,' he said. 'To beautiful Ellen. Beautiful, stunning Ellen!'

He took a mouthful of champagne and she did too, feeling the bubbles burst on her tongue, feeling a glow go through her that had nothing to do with champagne at all...

He smiled down at her. 'Tonight,' he told her, his mouth curving into an intimate smile, his lashes dipping over dark eyes lambent with expression, 'every man will envy me—you'll be a sensation.'

The word echoed in her head. A sudden memory stung like a wasp in her mind. She lowered her champagne glass, her fingers gripping it hard suddenly.

'Those girls—the stylists—they said you brought Tyla Brentley here last year—that *she* was a sensation.'

Max heard the sudden panic in her voice, that demon of self-doubt stabbing at her again. He wanted to kick it into touch without delay. He gave a deliberately dismissive shrug. 'Of course she was,' he said indifferently. 'Her fame guaranteed that. And Tyla adores men gazing at her. It flatters her insatiable vanity.'

Even as he spoke he knew his words were true. He, too, had once fed that vanity—until he'd realised that Tyla's self-absorption meant it was impossible for her to think of anyone but herself. His wealth had been useful to her, coming as it did with the person of a male whose looks could complement her own, and she had known with her innate instinct for self-publicity that she and he together made a couple that would always draw both eyes and attention, gaining precious press coverage to help her build her career. Tyla's belief in herself, in her own charm and beauty, had been total.

The very opposite of Ellen.

She was looking at him doubtfully still, as if she could not believe his indifference to having once squired a Hollywood film star. He wanted that doubt gone—completely—and so raised his champagne glass to his lips, deliberately letting his gaze wash over her.

'Tyla's got a good body—no doubt about that—but...' And now he let something else into his gaze that he knew from long experience had an effect on all females. 'But I can promise you that she had absolutely nothing on you. If Chloe,' he said 'is a tiny little Chihuahua...' he made his voice amused, deliberately exaggerating her stepsister's petiteness '...then Tyla is a...a gazelle, I guess. But *you*...' Once more his gaze rested on her, sending her the message he wanted... *needed*...her to get. 'You, Ellen, are a lioness!'

He grinned at her, and tilted his champagne glass to her in tribute.

'And lionesses gobble up little dogs and antelopes for breakfast!'

He toasted her again, his eyes becoming serious now, holding hers, sending home his essential message to her, the reassurance she needed— the reassurance that he would give her whatever it took. He would make sure of that. His eyes rested on her, their expression intent. Suddenly it seemed crucially important that Ellen believed him, and believed in her own newly revealed beauty. And it was for a reason that had nothing to do with his plans for Haughton. For a reason he was only dimly aware of—and yet it seemed to be forcing itself into his consciousness with an insistence he could not ignore.

I want it for her sake—not for mine. I want it so that she can be happy—happy in her own body, finally. I want that for her.

'Be proud of what you are,' he told her. 'Be happy in your body. Your fantastic body! Strong and lean and lithe—'

She felt gloved fingertips glide down the bare length of her upper arm.

'And with great muscle tone!' he finished approvingly.

Ellen's eyes flickered uncertainly. 'Maybe I need a shawl over my arms,' she ventured. 'I'm too muscular—'

Max rolled his eyes, shaking his head. 'Uh-uh! Remember—think lioness!' He let his gaze liquefy again, knowing the effect it would have, the effect he wanted right now. 'Think Artemis. Think goddess. Think beautiful…' There was a sudden husk in his voice that he had not put there deliberately at all, but which came of its own powerful accord. 'Very, very beautiful.'

The wash of his warm gaze over her was instinctive, and he felt it resonate with a warming of his blood, too, that surged in his body power-fully, unstoppably.

His eyes were holding hers, not letting her go. Ellen felt her breath catch in her breast, felt her heartbeat give a sudden surge, felt the surface of her skin tighten as if an electric charge were spreading out through its whole expanse, radiat-ing out from her quickened heart rate. She could feel her pupils flare, her lips part—felt faint, al-most, heard drumming in her ears…

The world seemed to slow down all around her.

And then the sound of the suite's doorbell ring-ing broke the moment. For a second Max just went on staring, unable to relinquish his gaze on the woman whose beauty he had revealed to her—and to himself. Then, with an exclamation in Greek, he dropped his hands, strode to the door and yanked it open.

As he saw who it was he relaxed immediately. 'Ah,' he said. 'Come in!'

Ellen turned, dazed, her pulse hectic, still blinking, breathless from that strange, powerful moment that had hummed like charged plasma between them. She saw a neatly suited man walk in, a briefcase handcuffed to his wrist. She blinked again. What on earth...?

'So,' she heard Max saying as the man set his briefcase on the table, unlocking it, 'what have you brought us?'

The man opened the lid and Ellen gasped audibly. It was jewellery, carefully nestled in black velvet liners, glittering in every hue—diamonds, emeralds, sapphires and rubies.

Rubies...

Ellen's eyes went to them immediately—it was impossible for them not to. She felt her breath draw in sharply as her gaze fixed on the ruby set, deep and glowing, a necklace, bracelet, earrings and a ring.

Max saw her focus on the set. Her expression was fixed, and for a second—just a second—he thought he saw something fleeting cross it, like a sudden convulsion. Then it was gone, and he was speaking.

'Ah, yes,' he said. 'Rubies, definitely. Ideal for your gown.'

The jeweller started to lift the pieces. 'As you can see,' he told them, 'their setting is of the period, and original. If I may...?'

He carefully lifted the necklace—a complex design of several loops of different lengths, with pendent rubies from each—and as he placed it around Ellen's throat the necklace occupied a considerable amount of the bare expanse of flesh between her throat and the swell of her breasts. He fastened the necklace, then held up a large hand mirror so she could see herself.

She gazed, her expression strange, and that fleeting look passed across her face again as she lifted her hand to touch the gems.

'Perfect,' said Max, well pleased. 'Let's get the rest of it on so we can see the final effect.'

Ellen still had that strange expression on her face. Max found himself wondering at it. He watched her hold out her wrist as the jeweller fastened the glittering bracelet around it and handed her the earrings. As he lifted the ring he paused, glancing doubtfully at Ellen's large hands.

'It will fit—just,' Ellen said.

She sounded sure of it and took the ring, pausing to glance at the inscription inside, which Max could see but not read, before carefully working the ring over her knuckle. It did, indeed, just fit—as she had forecast. She looked at it on her finger for a moment, the same strange, fixed expression on her face.

Then it was gone. She got to her feet. There was something different about her, Max fancied—some subtle change had come over her. There was an air of resolve about her—confidence, even. But then he was taking in the impact of her appearance, finished to perfection now with the glittering ruby parure that went so superbly with her Edwardian gown and hairstyle.

Beautiful!

That was the woman standing there, with her upswept hair, gems glittering, her toned, honed body sumptuously adorned with the lustrous ruby silk of her gown. He reached for his champagne glass and drained what was left, prompting Ellen to do likewise. They set their flutes down and Max turned to Ellen, holding out his arm to her.

'Time,' he said, and he gave her a little bow, his eyes glinting with pleasure and anticipation and appreciation, 'to take you to the ball.'

Walking into the hotel's ballroom, its rich red and gold decor a perfect complement to her black and ruby styling, Ellen tightened her hand on

Max's sleeve. Being at his side, she thought, her own generous figure seemed completely in proportion. His height easily topped hers by several inches—his wide shoulders and broad chest saw to that. Unconsciously, she seemed to straighten her shoulders further, and her hips moved with regal ease, her chin held high, as she walked beside Max with her athletic gait.

She should have felt nervous—but she didn't. Oh, the glass of champagne had helped, but it was not the bubbles in the champagne alone that were gliding her forward, filling her with wonder and elation.

She could see eyes going to her as they made their entrance, and for the first time in her life she experienced the oh-so-pleasurable thrill of knowing she was turning heads—for every reason a woman could dream of. Because she looked—*stunning.*

They both did.

As they walked past a mirror she caught their joint reflection and could see exactly why people were pausing to look at them. They were both tall, both sleekly groomed, with stunning looks, male *and* female, between them. Surely even

Max and the glamorous Tyla Brentley could not have turned more heads?

We make a fantastic couple!

The thought was in her head before she could stop it. Urgently she sought to suppress it, then gave in. Yes, she and Max *did* make a fantastic couple—but it was for tonight only, for the purposes of this glittering charity bash. That was what she had to remember. And one other vital thing.

He's only doing all this to soften me up—to try and persuade me to give up Haughton to him.

But even though she knew it was true she didn't seem to mind right now. How could she when what he'd given her this evening was something she had never thought she would ever possess in all her life? Freedom from the malign hex that Chloe had put on her so many years ago.

Self-knowledge flooded through her, washing away so much of the blindness that had clouded her image of herself for so long. The blindness that she had allowed her stepsister to inflict on her.

I let Chloe have that power over me. I let her

control my mind, my image of myself, my sense of worth.

It seemed so strange to her now, to think of how defiant she'd always been with Pauline and her daughter—and yet they had controlled her at this most basic, potent level. But no longer— never again! A sense of power, of newborn confidence swept through her. Unconsciously she lifted her fingers to the necklace, touching the jewels around her throat. Beautiful jewels to adorn a beautiful woman. A woman worthy of a man like Max Vasilikos.

She looked up at him now, easily a head taller than her, and smiled. He caught her expression and answered it with his own. Long lashes swept down over his eyes and he patted the hand hooked into his.

'Enjoy,' said Max, smiling down at her.

And enjoy she did. That was the amazement of it all.

Time and again her fingers brushed at her necklace, or grazed the gold band around her finger beneath its ruby setting—and every time she did she gave a little smile, half haunting, half joyous.

As Max had promised her, sitting to her left she

found one of the host charity's directors, who listened attentively as she told him about the camps she ran, then nodded approvingly and told Ellen he'd be happy to help with her funding.

Glowing, she turned to Max. 'Thank you!' she exclaimed, and it was heartfelt.

And she was not just thanking him for setting her up with this funding, or his cheque for fifteen thousand pounds. It was for lifting Chloe's curse from her shoulders—setting her free from it.

His eyes met hers and, half closed, half veiled, they flickered very slightly. As if he were thinking about something but not telling her. He raised his glass of wine to her.

'Here's to a better future for you,' he murmured.

The corner of his mouth pulled into a quizzical smile, and she answered with one of her own in return, lifting her glass too.

'A better future,' she echoed softly.

At the edge of her consciousness Haughton loomed, still haunted by Pauline and Chloe, the dilemma insoluble. But the house she loved so much, the home that she longed only to be safe, seemed far, far away right now. Real—much more real—was this moment...this extraordinary present she was experiencing. All thanks to Max, the man who had made it possible for her.

For an instant her gaze held his, and she felt bathed and warmed by the deep, dark brown of eyes fringed by thick lashes, flecked with gold. And then for an even briefer instant, so brief she could only wonder whether it had been real, there was a sudden change in them, a sudden, scorching intimacy.

She sheared her gaze away, feeling her heart jolt within her as if an electric shock had just kicked it. As if it were suddenly hard to breathe.

All through the rest of the meal, and the speeches and the fundraising auction afterwards, she could feel the echo of that extraordinary jolt to her heartbeat, flickering in her consciousness as port and liqueurs, coffee and petit fours circulated. Then, on the far side of the grand ballroom an orchestra started up.

'Oh, how lovely!' she exclaimed as the music went into the lilting strains of a slow waltz, ideal for an Edwardian-themed ball.

'It's Lehár!' exclaimed one of the women at their table, delighted.

'So it is!' agreed Ellen, starting to hum the composer's familiar melody—the waltz from *The Merry Widow* operetta.

'Well, I think this calls for audience participation,' said the charity director at her side, as all around them at the other tables guests were getting to their feet to take to the dance floor. 'Will you do me the honour?' he asked Ellen with a smile.

But he was forestalled. Max was standing up.

'I claim the first waltz,' he said, catching Ellen's elbow and guiding her to her feet. His rival conceded gracefully. Max bore Ellen off.

She was in a state of consternation, aware that her heart was racing and that she felt breathless. Taken over.

But then Max has taken me over all day, hasn't he? I've done everything he wanted, all the time!

Well, now she was going to dance with him, and she wasn't getting a choice about it. Except—

'I have *no* idea how to waltz!' she exclaimed. 'And I think the Viennese waltz is different from the English waltz anyway. And I—'

He cut her short. 'Follow my lead,' he instructed, and simply took her into his arms and swept her off.

Into the dance.

Into the irresistible, lilting music that wafted them around the ballroom floor.

She felt her long, heavy silk skirts become as light as a feather, swirling around her legs as Max whirled her around until she was dizzy with it, until all she could do was clutch helplessly at his shoulder, hang on to his hand for dear life as he turned her and guided her and never, never let her go.

'You see? It's easy.' He smiled at her. 'Much easier than you feared.'

And she knew, with a little skip of her heart, that it was not just the waltzing he meant.

It's all been so, so easy. The lifting of the hex. Her transformation tonight. Putting on this gorgeous costume, being swept away in his arms...

Joy filled her—a wonderful sense of carefree elation as if, simply by whirling her around like this, he had whisked away all that oppressed her.

And for tonight he has! I know that I will have to go home tomorrow, back to all the difficulties and the stress and the fear of losing Haughton. But for tonight I will waltz my cares away.

The music ended with a flourish, and the cessation of the swirling made her head spin instead. But then she was joining with the others in applauding the orchestra, its players in historical costume as well, and their leader was turning and bowing, introducing the next dance they were going to play.

It was a polka, and Ellen's eyes widened again.

Max didn't let her speak. 'Just follow my lead,' he instructed again.

And once more she did. It was just as well, she thought absently, that she was pretty fit, for the dance was vigorous and not a few couples finished panting. But Max wasn't the slightest out of breath, and neither was she.

'Thank goodness for early-morning runs!' she exclaimed.

'It's hot work, this elegant dancing,' Max agreed, running a finger around his distinctly damp collar.

Ellen smiled. 'My father used to say that *his* father, when they went to dances before the war, had to take spare collars with him because they wilted during the night.'

Max laughed. 'Well, I envy you your bare shoulders and arms, I can tell you. Will it cause a scandal if I shed this very hot evening jacket, I wonder?'

'You'll be blackballed instantly!' she warned him with a laugh.

'Oh, well, I'm just a foreigner and a parvenu, so I won't care,' he riposted, and took her back into his arms as the music started up again.

It was a much slower waltz now, and Ellen was relieved. Or at least she was until she felt Max's hand tightening at her waist. It was hard to feel much through the whalebone bodice, but there was something in the way he was imprinting his hold on her that made her breath catch despite the slowness of the music. Made it catch again when she saw the expression in his eyes, looking down at her. She felt colour run out into her cheeks. She tried to stop it, tried to hope that he would take it only for heat, no other reason. She tried to pull her gaze away, but it was hopeless...

'Glad you came to the ball?' he asked, a faint smile ghosting at his mouth.

His long lashes swept down over his eyes and he smiled at her. Were there gold flecks in those eyes? She could only gaze into their depths, captivated and entranced.

Her lips parted in a wide, joyful smile. 'Oh, yes! It's just...*wonderful*! All of it. Every bit!'

A wicked glint gleamed in Max's eyes. 'Even the whalebone in your bodice?' he asked.

'OK,' she allowed. 'Not that.'

'Though it *does* give you the most superb figure,' he said, and now...oh, most definitely...now there were golden flecks in his eyes.

He pulled a little away from her so his eyes could take in the glory of her narrowed waist, the full roundness of her hips, and then, moving upwards, the generous curvature of her breasts. His gaze lingered...then he dragged them away.

No. The voice inside his head was stern. No, he must not. This evening was about liberating Ellen Mountford from the chains that weighed her down. Freeing her from the mental burdens that blighted her life, made her want to hide herself away in her safe place, her childhood home, where she could moulder away, never emerging into the world.

Well, she was emerging now, all right. Male eyes were all over her. Max had seen that the moment he'd walked into the ballroom. They were on her still, and he didn't blame them.

Mine are too...

No. The stern voice inside his head came again. No—he must not permit that. This evening was for *her*, not him! Oh, it was for himself too— of course it was—but only because showing Ellen how wonderful her life could be once she joined the world, instead of hiding herself away at Haughton, would mean that he could acquire what he was set on acquiring. Which was not Ellen Mountford—it was the house she would not willingly sell to him.

But you could have her as well...

The siren thought was in his head, as sinuous and seductive as the slow pulse of the music he was moving to.

Ellen was in his arms, her body so close to his, her weight pressing in on him as they turned, his arm around her waist, her rich ruby mouth smiling up at him. Tempting him...

The music ended and he was glad. He led her back to their table and immediately the charity director was on his feet. Ellen was led away, and Max watched her go. Was there a reluctance in her now? Would she rather have not danced again but sat with him and watched the dancers? He didn't know—knew only that there was a kind of growl inside him…a growl that made him reach for the cognac bottle and pour himself a glass.

The two other couples at the table were taking a break as well, and were chatting, drawing him into their conversation. He joined in civilly but his gaze, he knew, kept going back out to the dance floor, searching for Ellen.

I want her.

That was the voice in his head now. Stark, blunt and simple. His jaw set. He could want her all he liked, but fulfilling that want would lead to complications.

The question was—did he care?

And right now, watching her in another man's arms—this woman he'd released from the bondage of her mental chains, freed to revel in the natural beauty that was hers—and feeling that deep, primal growl rising in him again, he knew as the fiery liqueur glazed his throat and fuelled his heated blood that he didn't care at all…

CHAPTER SEVEN

THE WORLD WAS whirling pleasantly around her—oh, so pleasantly! Ellen felt herself swaying slightly, as if she were still dancing, humming a waltz tune, hearing her long silk skirts rustling. The ball was over, midnight long gone, and now she was back up in the penthouse suite. The orchestra was still playing in her head. And everything was wonderful! Oh, just *wonderful*! Her gown was wonderful, her hair was wonderful, the dancing had been wonderful, the evening had been wonderful!

Max had been wonderful...

She gazed at him now, blood singing in her veins. He was twisting open a bottle of water, looking so tall, so strong, so utterly devastating in his Edwardian evening dress, and her eyes just drank him in as the room swirled around her and the music played in her head and on her lips. All she wanted to do, all she longed to do, was to be back in his arms, dancing and dancing…

'Drink this—and drink it all,' Max's deep voice instructed her as he came to her and handed her a large glass of water. 'You'll thank me in the morning, I promise you.'

'I feel fine,' she said. 'Absolutely fine.' Still, she gulped down the water, never taking her gaze from Max—wonderful, *wonderful* Max!

How gorgeous he is—how incredibly handsome and gorgeous and wonderful and devastating and…

Then she yawned—a huge, exhausted yawn. Her eyes blinked.

'Time for bed,' said Max.

But not, alas, with him. He knew that. The champagne, the wine, the liqueurs she'd drunk made that out of the question. Should he regret it? He shouldn't, he knew, but he did all the same.

Maybe it's for the best. That was what he needed to tell himself. Remind himself of all the complications that might arise were he to follow what he knew his body wanted right now…the new-found desire that had swept over him.

I want to celebrate her new-found freedom with

her. I want to take the final step of her liberation with her. I want to be the man who does that—

Well, not tonight. Frustration could bite at him all it liked, but that was that. And he—he'd be back in his own bedroom in the hotel suite, heading for a cold shower.

But first he had a real ordeal to get through. One that was going to test him to the limits.

'Hold still!' he instructed her, catching the back of her shoulders to steady her.

It was a mistake, for the warmth of her bare skin under his palms was an unwise sensation for him to feel right now. He pulled his hands away as if burnt, made his fingers drop down to the fastenings of her dress instead. *Thee mou*, there were a million of them! As he started the finicky work of undoing them he could feel the effort of not thinking about what he was doing.

Don't think about how her beautiful bare back is emerging...how she's dropped her head, exposing the tender nape of her neck caressed by tendrils of her chestnut hair...how easy...how tempting it would be to lower your mouth and graze that delicate skin with your lips. No, don't think about any of that—

He swallowed heavily, dropping his hands away. 'Done!'

She turned, oblivious to the punishing, disciplined self-control he was exerting, her unfastened bodice held up only by her hands pressed to her half-exposed breasts, her feathered shoulder straps collapsing down her arms as well. A sigh of happiness, of bliss escaped her, and her eyes were clinging to his.

'This has been,' she announced, 'the most *wonderful* night of my life.'

Her lips were parted, her eyes glowing, her face lifted up to his. She swayed towards him in the motion of a dance, with intoxication in her blood, unconscious invitation in her glorious goddess body.

And he was lost. Totally, completely lost. Could resist her no longer.

His hands fastened on her upper arms and he hauled her to him. Drew her smiling parted lips to his and took his fill. He could not resist it— just could not.

Tasting first, he glided his lips across the velvet softness of hers, taking possession of her mouth, tasting her bouquet like a rich, radiant wine. Then, as his kiss deepened, he opened his mouth to hers and she came with him—came with him every iota of the way—moving her mouth on his, opening to him, tasting him, taking her fill of him.

He could feel her full breasts pressing against the cotton of his shirtfront, feel her nipples start to peak, feel desire flare through her, fuelled by the wine in her blood, the champagne in her veins, the music in her head.

Hunger for her leapt in him, seared through him. He knew his body was surging, engorging, knew that desire and need and all that could burn like an inferno between a man and a woman was igniting within him now. Knew that in seconds the conflagration would take hold—unstoppable, unquenchable.

With a groan, he let her go, wrenching his mouth from hers, pulling his hands away, stepping back from her.

There was a dazed expression on her face, the bewilderment of loss in her eyes—her huge, widened eyes—and their pupils were flaring with desire, arousal...

He shook his head. Held up his hands. Stepped further back.

'Goodnight!' he said.

His voice was shaken, he could hear it, and he could feel the heat in his body still, the fullness still there, but he had to beat it back, subdue it. Whatever primal hunger was possessing him, he had to defeat it. To indulge himself now, when far too much wine and champagne was coursing through her, would be unforgivable.

For a second a stricken look was there in her eyes—a look that somehow pierced him like a stiletto blade in his throat—and then, like the sun coming out from a cloud, dazzling in its brightness, she smiled. Her face lit up once more.

'Goodnight!' she breathed. 'Oh, *goodnight!*'

He backed to the door. He did not want to do this. Did not want to leave. But he had to. Had to get back to his room—had to get that cold shower sluicing down over his body...*had* to!

As he reached the door she lifted her hand from one side of her bodice, dangerously exposing yet more of her sweet, succulent flesh, a final torment for him, and then, with another dazzling smile, an insouciant, joyous gesture, she kissed her fingers and blew the kiss to him.

'Thank you!'

They were the last words he heard before he got out through the door and pulled it shut, to keep him safe.

Safe from the only thing in the world he wanted to do right now...

Go right back in and sweep her into his arms.

Ellen was asleep, but someone was making her wake up. A hand was on her shoulder, gently shaking her. She shrugged it off, nestled back down into her pillows, but the hand returned. Someone said something to her, but she didn't know what. It was foreign. Greek?

Greek!

She bolted upright, only just having the presence of mind to clutch her bedclothes to her, her eyes flaring open. Max Vasilikos, freshly showered—she could tell from the damp hair feathering his forehead and the towelling robe that emphasised the Mediterranean tan of his skin—was sitting on her bed.

'How are you feeling?' he enquired. His voice was urbane, equable—and amused.

She pushed her hair out of her face. It seemed to her to be softer than it usually was, and finer, and less heavy. She blinked, looking around her, dragging her gaze past the figure of the man sitting at the foot of the bed, with his dark eyes resting on her speculatively and a curve at his sculpted mouth that suddenly made her very, *very* aware of her state of dishevelment.

'Um—fine,' she got out.

Was she fine? she wondered. She blinked. Yes, she did seem to be OK. Memory came rushing back, tumbling into her head like a series of snapshots. The ball—that fantastic, gorgeous, wonderful ball! Chatting away to all those people over dinner. Dancing with Max.

Kissing Max...

Colour flared in her cheeks as memory flooded her, intense and vivid.

He kissed me! Max Vasilikos—the man who made me beautiful and waltzed the night away with me!

Max saw the colour flare and knew what she was thinking. It was what he was only too conscious of himself. His night had not been peaceful. It had been disturbed by dreams. Dreams in which there had been no need to tear himself away from the woman he'd been kissing.

No—don't think about it now! Not when he was sitting on her bed and she was only a metre away from him, her naked body shielded only by the sheet she was clutching to her, her lush hair tumbling wantonly around her shoulders, her smeared mascara making her eyes smoky and deep...

He got to his feet, stepping away from the bed. Well away. 'I've ordered brunch,' he told her. 'So have a wake-up shower and come on through.'

She nodded, and waited till he was well clear of the room before getting up.

It was strange, she thought as she caught her reflection in the mirror of the en-suite bathroom... She was so used to her body, so used to thinking it large and muscular and unattractive. And yet now— Her eyes held her own naked reflection. Saw it for the very first time not through Chloe's eyes, but through someone else's completely.

Max's eyes...

Tall, with sculpted shoulders, taut arms, gener-

ous breasts, flat abs, toned glutes, strong quads, long legs. A goddess body?

And her face still held the beauty conjured from it by those skilful magic-making stylists last night. Her fingers lifted uncertainly to her hair. Whatever those chattering women had done to it, it was amazing. Its colour was so much richer, glowing in the lights around the vanity unit, and it felt so light on her head, yet it waved in lush tresses down over her shoulders, softening her face, her jaw, caressing her neck. She touched her mouth with her fingertips—elongated nails still crimson with varnish—and felt a smile part her mouth.

A goddess indeed...

She heard Max's words in her head, felt his eyes on her, his hand on her spine as they'd waltzed.

The melody played in her head again. Happiness filled her. Whatever her worries, whatever her woes, this...*this* would always be with her now.

He made me beautiful.

He might be trying to take her beloved home from her, but he had given her something she had never thought to have—something that Chloe's cruelty had taken from her, that her own self-doubt, self-criticism had *let* her stepsister take from her.

And Max—wonderful, wonderful Max!—had now restored it to her.

With a smile of wonder and gratitude still playing on her lips she piled her hair up, pinned it loosely, and stepped into the shower unit. Brunch beckoned—and so did the thought of seeing Max again.

Even if only for what was left of the morning.

A pang smote her. She swallowed as the hot water plunged down over her shoulders, rousing her to full wakefulness. Suddenly the thought of leaving him, of returning home to Haughton, seemed like the worst thing in the world.

But the ball is over—and it's time to go home.

For the first time in her life she did not want to.

Max was already seated at the table when Ellen emerged. He was clad, like her, in a white towelling robe. Seeing him like that seemed suddenly very...intimate.

Into her head came the memory, vivid and real, of how he had kissed her.

Oh, she might have been intoxicated—with champagne and wine, with music and wonder—but that could not dim the searing memory.

Instantly she reproved herself fiercely.

It was just a kiss! Don't make anything of it! It was only a kiss. It meant nothing—just a way to say goodnight.

Yet even as she told herself that she could feel the colour flare in her face. Busily, she sat herself down, hoping Max hadn't seen. Didn't know the reason for it.

It would have meant nothing to him—think how many women he's kissed in his life! With looks like his...

And one of those women—the most recent—had been a film star. To a man used to kissing film stars—used to doing a whole lot more than kissing!—bestowing a goodnight kiss on *her* was...well, nothing.

But not to me.

Her eyes flickered a moment. No, it had not been nothing to her...

To me his kiss was the ultimate breaking of Chloe's vicious hex. The one I gave in to—was too cowed to fight, to deny. I gave her an easy victory. A victory she revelled in!

Her expression steeled. But no more. Chloe's cruel mental domination of her was over. She had to keep it that way.

She looked across at Max. His eyes were resting on her with an expression in them that was half glinting, half veiled. She met it square-on, refusing to let any self-conscious memory colour her cheeks. Then she looked at the lavish brunch spread out before her. She was instantly hungry.

'Mmm…eggs Benedict. My favourite,' she announced appreciatively.

She took a generous helping and got stuck in. Max was doing likewise—well, he had a big frame to fill, and muscle burned more calories than fat…not that there was a trace of fat about him. He was lean and powerful and devastatingly attractive, and the way the tan of his skin contrasted with the white of his robe, the way there was really quite a lot of chest exposed in the deep vee…

She gulped silently and focussed on her food.

'No sign of a hangover?' Max enquired. She didn't look hungover in the slightest, and she shook her head, making her long wavy tresses resettle on her shoulders and waft around her cheeks. He felt satisfaction go through him. Those stylists had been worth their weight in gold! Even with all the make-up now scrubbed off, the changes they'd made were glaringly noticeable—most of all the taming of her fearsome, frowning monobrow.

She wasn't frowning now at all. 'Nope,' she said. 'All that water you poured into me before I flaked out did the trick!'

'I told you you'd thank me in the morning,' he replied with a glint in his eyes.

She made herself look at him, pausing in her eating. 'I *do* thank you,' she said 'I thank you for...for everything!'

She didn't have to spell it out. He knew. He smiled at her down the length of the table. Then raised his glass of orange juice to her. 'To the new you, Ellen—and may the old one be banished for good!

He took a draught of the juice, setting down the glass. 'Now,' he opened, sounding business-like, 'what we need to get done today is sorting out your wardrobe. Fabulous though you look in

Edwardian costume, it's not for every day,' he finished lightly, with another smile. 'So, when we've eaten it'll be time to go shopping.'

A troubled look shadowed her face. 'I really need to go home,' she said.

Max raised his eyebrows. 'What for? It's not term-time—'

'Yes, but… Well…I really ought to…'

He gave an airy wave of his hand. No way was Ellen going to beetle off back to Haughton and bury herself there again! Not yet—not by a long way! He hadn't done with her…

Deep in his abdomen he felt an oh-so-masculine response kick in. He'd had to relinquish her last night—anything else would have been inexcusable—but the impulse he'd experienced then, the overriding rush of desire, had in no way been attenuated. His mind was made up—the long, sleepless, frustrated hours of the night he'd just spent had given him conviction of that.

A romance is exactly what she needs. It will show her how wonderful life can be if she just emerges from her shell, tastes all that life can offer now that she knows how beautiful she is. She can start to shed the burden of bitter resent-

ment, knowing that her deep, dark, disturbing jealousy and envy of her stepsister is quite unnecessary.

And with that burden of resentment lifted— well, then she wouldn't need to keep trying to thwart Pauline and Chloe by refusing to sell her share of Haughton. Wouldn't need to keep trying to punish Pauline for marrying her father and Chloe for having the beauty she thought she herself was denied.

'So,' he said decisively, 'it's all settled. There's absolutely no call for you to head off straight away, so we'll definitely go shopping.'

She was still looking at him with a troubled expression. She wanted to tell him that even if she didn't actually need to go back home today shopping for clothes was the last thing she could afford. Her salary was wiped out paying for her living expenses and Pauline and Chloe's extravagances! But even as she thought it she felt rebellion stir. If *they* could fund their lavish lifestyle by selling off paintings from Haughton, well, so could she!

In the deep pocket of her robe she could feel the weight of the jewellery she'd worn last night, which she would hand back to Max as she must, however reluctantly...

A stab of anger bit at her, hardening her resolve. Her expression changed as she made her decision. Max saw it and was glad.

He was even more glad, later that afternoon, when she emerged from the changing room of one of the most upmarket fashion houses, finally looking the way her natural looks deserved.

It hadn't been completely plain sailing—she'd balked as they'd walked in, a look of near panic on her face, and he'd had to steer her firmly towards the serried racks of clothes.

'I don't think there'll be anything to fit me!' she'd said nervously, her eyes casting about at the stick-thin customers who all seemed to be Chloe clones.

Doubt had suddenly assailed her. She'd been wearing, perforce, the dowdy old-fashioned suit she'd worn yesterday, and there, surrounded by elegance and fashion, she'd felt her fragile new-found confidence waver. Panic had bitten at her throat.

They're all looking at me—wondering what

on earth a lumpy frump like me is doing here! Wanting me to get out, to stop inflicting myself on their eyesight!

The old, painful, mortifying self-consciousness had come back, drowning her, trying to send a tide of humiliated colour back into her face. The urge to run out of the shop, to take herself off to the station, to rush back down to Haughton, seeking its refuge, hiding there in solitude, safe from condemning eyes, had almost overpowered her.

Then Max had spoken, ignoring her protestation. 'This will suit you,' he'd said decisively, reaching for a knee-length dress in warm caramel, soft jersey with a draped neckline. 'And these.'

He'd taken a teal-blue dress and a tailored jacket off the rack. He'd handed them to her and then started sorting through the trousers, pulling out a black pair and a chestnut-brown pair, before picking up a couple of cashmere sweaters. He'd guided her to the changing rooms.

'In you go,' he'd said, and he'd given her the rest of the clothes and a gentle push. He'd had no intention of letting those chains start winding themselves around her mind again.

As she had headed, still reluctantly but obedi- ently, into the changing rooms he'd beckoned to a sales assistant, giving her a particularly engaging smile. 'We're going to need a lot more clothes,' he'd said, nodding at Ellen's back.

The sales assistant had cast an expert eye over her, taking in the tight, ill-fitting suit. 'Definitely.' She had nodded and glided off, returning with a large selection of separates, plus shoes, belts and some costume jewellery.

With a smile at Max, who'd settled himself comfortably into one of the leather chairs con- veniently placed nearby for attendant males, complete with magazines about cars and fitness to while away their time while they waited for their womenfolk, she had whisked them into the changing room.

It had taken quite some time for Ellen to emerge...

CHAPTER EIGHT

'TELL ME,' MAX SAID, 'how are you with heli-copters?'

Ellen stared. 'Helicopters?'

'Yes. I've got one on standby,' he informed her. 'There's a property out in the Chilterns I want to take a quick look at, and a helicopter is the fast-est way.'

'I've never been in one,' Ellen said.

Max grinned. 'Great—a new experience. You'll love it.'

He bore her off towards the kerb, where his car was hovering. He wasn't giving her a chance to object, just as he hadn't given her a chance to run out of that fashion house. When she'd finally emerged from the changing room he'd wanted to punch the air, like he had the night before. And now she had looked—fantastic!

Straw-coloured trousers neatly hugged her trim hips, and a casual cashmere sweater in oatmeal superbly moulded her generous breasts. A long jacket and a swish leather handbag completed the outfit.

Behind her came the sales assistant, with more clothes, and they all totted up to a good half-dozen or more capacious carrier bags.

His driver climbed out of the car to put the bags in the boot as Max helped Ellen into the back of the car.

She was in a daze—no doubt about it. She'd handed over her credit card, wincing at the huge total, but then tightening her mouth in defiance. Another watercolour would have to be sold—but this time *she* would get the benefit of it.

And it was money well spent—she'd seen that the moment she'd taken in her reflection, seeing not frumpy, lumpy Elephant Ellen but a tall, good-looking, athletic, fashionably dressed woman who could stride through the world with assurance and poise. It was a good feeling—a brilliant feeling!

A bubble of happiness rose in her, as if she'd just drunk a glass of champagne. She was going to enjoy this—enjoy *everything*! Including the novelty of a ride in a helicopter.

Her eyes widened in excitement as the noisy machine rose into the air, skating high above the River Thames. London became increasingly miniature, and then was left behind as the countryside approached. She gazed spellbound as they flew, then circled over the property Max wanted to assess.

It was another large country house, Victorian gothic in style, and far larger than Haughton. Only then did a shadow cross her eyes, for it reminded her of the danger to her home. Oh, he could buy anywhere he liked—so why insist on buying the one place in the world she so desperately loved?

Conflicting emotions swirled in her. Max had been so *good* to her, and even though she knew why he was doing it, it did not detract from the gift he had given her.

I will always, always be grateful to him.

It was a gratitude she voiced yet again that evening, as they dined in the Michelin-starred restaurant at the hotel.

'All I've done, Ellen,' he said, and smiled, 'is show you what was always there—that's all.

You've always been like this—but you hid it. And now you don't any more. It's as simple as that.'

His eyes washed over her, liking what they saw. She was wearing the teal-blue dress he'd instinctively known would suit her, and it did—much to his satisfaction—and her hair was loosely gathered into a chignon at the back of her head. Her make-up—another purchase that day—was not as striking as it had been for the ball, but it gave her smoky eyes and long lashes and a soft, tender mouth...

He dragged his gaze away, returning to his study of the wine list. The arrival of the sommelier diverted him some more, and when he was done with his discussion and selection he turned back—to find Ellen looking around the dining room and getting the attention from male diners that she well deserved. He was glad to see it—it would do her good.

All the same, he reached out to touch her arm, with an atavistic instinct to show the other males she was spoken for.

Her gaze came back to him. 'So, will you buy that place you looked at this afternoon?' she asked.

As she'd glanced around the room she'd become conscious that she was being looked at by other men, and whilst it had given her a little thrill of confidence in her new appearance it had also, with her not being used to it, been somewhat disconcerting. She was grateful to have Max with her. He seemed...reassuring.

How odd that Max Vasilikos should seem reassuring to me—yet it's true.

A thought flickered through her mind. Could this man who had wrought this seismic revolution within her, with whom she'd spent the most amazing twenty-four hours in her life and still counting, really be the same man who was threatening Haughton, threatening to wrest from her all that she held most dear? It was hard to think of it.

'Maybe.' He was answering her now. 'Of course I'll need to look over it in person. But it ticks a lot of boxes. It's on at a good price, I like the look of it and it's close to London.'

'Much closer than Haughton!' she heard herself say quickly.

Max's eyes veiled. 'Haughton is quite different,' he said. 'I have...*other* plans for it.'

'*If* you manage to buy it!' Ellen riposted, her chin going up.

But even as she spoke she wished she hadn't. She didn't want to talk about Haughton, about how he wanted to buy it. For now—just for now—she only wanted to enjoy the present, this wonderful time with him. Nothing more than that. All the difficult, painful stuff could be left to one side. For now at least.

He gave a guarded smile. 'As you say,' he murmured, offering nothing more than that.

The sommelier returned with his choice of wine and he busied himself sampling it, nodding his approval.

He glanced across at Ellen. 'So,' he said, 'did you enjoy the helicopter ride?'

'It was amazing!' she exclaimed. 'A completely new experience.'

His long lashes dipped over his dark eyes. 'Well, new experiences are what you *should* be having, Ellen. Lots and lots of amazing new experiences!'

Was there a subtext to what he was saying? He was conscious of it. He was determined for her to have experiences with him... But he also wanted to indicate to her how her life could, and would, open up once she was free—not just of the chains that had made her think herself plain and unattractive, but of those that bound her to a house that had become a weapon against her stepmother and stepsister.

'Tell me,' he said, taking the subject further, 'when were you last abroad?'

She thought. 'Um...I took a school team to the Netherlands in the autumn term,' she recollected. 'And I did a field trip to Iceland with some sixth-formers—that was extraordinary. The geology and geography is breathtaking!'

Skilfully Max drew her out, and then equally skilfully drew her into contemplating where in the world she might yet like to go, exchanging his own views and experiences with her as their food arrived and they started on their meal.

An idea was forming in his head, but it would be premature to voice it now. He *could* sound her out, however, in general...

'And what about sun, sea and sand—tropical beaches and all that?' he ventured. 'Or did you do all that as a child in holidays with your parents?'

She shook her head. 'No, my mother preferred

cultural destinations—so I've been to places like Florence and Paris and so on. Done all the museums and art galleries. I'm not sure I'd like to go back to those places again,' she said. 'They'd have sad memories for me now.' A shadowed look permeated her expression.

He nodded in sympathy. 'I've never gone back to where I was raised except once. And that,' he said, 'was to buy out the *taverna* my mother once slaved away in. I bought it, and now run it as a place to train unemployed young men—of which Greece now sadly has all too many—in useful skills.'

She looked at him. 'Would you never live in Greece again? Never settle there?'

He shook his head. 'I've let it go, Ellen. Cut my ties to a painful past and made a new life for myself. A better life by far! One I'd never known I'd dreamed of until I started to make the dream come true.' His eyes rested on her, his expression intent, challenging. 'Maybe, Ellen, it's time for you to do the same. Make a new life for yourself. Think about the future instead of clinging to a past that is gone.'

He'd spoken deliberately. It had to be said, after all. For her own sake as well as his.

She needs to be free—free of her chains. Free to move on. She needs to see the truth of that.

But a mutinous look had closed down her face and her eyes dropped, refusing to meet his gaze. 'This isn't a subject for discussion,' she said tersely. 'I don't want to sell you Haughton and that's that.'

Inside her head thoughts were teeming. She was immediately wary, reminding herself just who this man was and why he was interested in her, in spending time with her.

He's a stranger who wants to buy your home— and he'll use any means to get it. Including all this that he's doing for you now. Oh, he may have given you a priceless gift, freeing you from what that witch Chloe did for so long, but don't think it's for your sake he's done it—it's for his. That's why he's done it.

From the corner of her eye she saw the waiter approaching with their dessert and was glad of the diversion.

For a moment Max went on gazing at her, fulminating. Her constant obdurate stonewalling was frustrating. Then, with an intake of breath, he let it go. He'd made his point—he would let it be. He hoped she would take it on board internally, even if she did not accept it yet. Besides, he thought as he rested his gaze on her closed face as she doggedly focussed on her food, he wanted to dismiss the subject himself. He didn't want to think about the house she was refusing to sell, or her convoluted reasons for that. No, what he wanted to think about right now was something far more immediate.

The effect that she was having on his libido.

He'd been resolutely repressing it all day, but now, sitting opposite her, with her newly revealed beauty playing havoc with his senses, he knew without a doubt what he wanted to happen between them.

Even if she didn't own a single brick of the house I want to buy from her I'd still be doing this—still be spending the day with her, the evening with her.

And the night too...?

His eyes drifted over her face, visually caressing the curve of her cheek, the length of her lashes, the sweep of her hair, the lush, inviting richness of her mouth whose sweetness he had tasted so tormentingly as he'd bade her good-night. He tore his gaze away, only for it to slip downwards, to see how the soft material of her dress shaped and pulled across the generous swell of her breasts, and into his head leapt the memory of how they had danced last night, her body so intimately close to his. He wanted to feel her in his arms again, closer and closer still...

He reached for his glass of wine, started to speak again to take his mind back into safer territory for the moment. Besides, he wanted to remove that fixed, closed look on her face. Wanted to see it soften again, become animated with interest and engagement with him. Wanted to see her smile at him again.

'So, tell me,' he opened decisively, 'this eco-resort of mine in the Caribbean—do you think it's the kind of place that would appeal to someone keen on an active holiday?'

It was a deliberate trail—something to catch her attention, make her look at him, take her away from that dark mental interior where she brooded on her father's resented second marriage. It seemed to work, for she lifted her head, blinking for a moment.

'What sort of activities will there be?' she asked.

Max waved a hand expansively. 'Well, water sports, definitely. Nothing motorised—that would be out of keeping—but sailing, windsurfing, kayaking…that sort of thing. Snorkelling and scuba diving, of course—the reef is notable, and I'm hiring a marine ecologist to advise me on the best way to preserve and nurture it. All the sports will have to be outdoors, but to be honest there probably isn't room for a tennis court. Plus it would require a hard surface—again, out of keeping. We'd run beach volleyball maybe,' he finished.

He found himself on the receiving end of an old-fashioned look. 'Well, that would be popular as a *spectator* sport—for the male guests, certainly,' she commented drily.

Max's riposte was immediate. 'It would be popular with me if *you* were taking part, even more certainly.'

The sweep of his long lashes over his revealing glance gave him the satisfaction of seeing her dip her gaze as his compliment registered. He followed through seamlessly.

'So, does it tempt you to come out and check over the place yourself? Try everything out before the first guests arrive later in the season?'

Ellen stared at him. 'Go to the Caribbean?' she said, as if he'd suggested a jaunt to Mars.

Max lifted a hand nonchalantly. 'Why not? You've got time before term starts again, haven't you? Plenty of time to cross the Atlantic.'

She opened her mouth, then closed it again. Gave a slight shake of her head as if that was all she could manage. He let it go. He'd planted the idea—he would harvest it later. When the time was right.

He started to talk about coral reef conservation. It was as good a subject to pass the time as any. He was enjoying the meal, enjoying spending this convivial time with her—no doubt about that. And there was even less doubt that he was looking forward to what he wanted to happen afterwards...

The elevator, when they walked into it some time later, seemed too small, too empty. And as it whooshed them up to the top floor of the hotel Ellen could feel her stomach dropping away. But it was not just from the effect of the lift. No, it was caused by the man she was sharing it with.

He stood a few feet away from her and gave her a quick smile as the doors opened, waiting for her to emerge. The soft, deep carpet of the penthouse-level corridor muffled all sound. It was completely deserted. A strange sensation of electricity started to run in her veins, along her nerve fibres, just as it had throughout dinner, in little jolts and quivers, every time she'd let her eyes rest on him.

Inside the suite, only a table lamp was lit, creating an atmosphere that was…intimate.

'Nightcap?' Max asked, strolling towards the drinks cabinet.

For a second—just a second—Ellen heard in her head the answer that she could give—*should* give. *Thank you, but no. It's been a long day. I really must turn in.* But instead she heard her voice saying, 'Lovely.'

She walked to the sofa. She could feel her heart thumping in heavy slugs, feel that electric current setting off again, humming through her veins.

Carefully she lowered herself down, deliberately kicking off her shoes, tucking her legs under her and resting her elbow on the sofa's arm. A moment later Max was placing a small measure of liqueur on the coffee table in front of the sofa and then lowering himself on to the far end, his free hand cupping a cognac glass. It was a large sofa, but it suddenly felt very, very small.

She took a tiny sip of the sweet, orange-scented fiery liquid—no more than a sip, for it was strong, she knew, and she'd already drunk wine at dinner. A supreme sense of self-consciousness filled her—but not like anything she'd ever known before. This was nothing like the embarrassingly awkward consciousness of her ungainly body, her unlovely appearance that she was so bitterly used to feeling.

No—this was utterly different.

A lioness—that's what he called me last night!

And that was what she felt like—with her lithe body toned and honed, not an ounce of excess fat on it, yet rounded and womanly. She was supremely conscious of the way her hip was indenting the cushions of the sofa, the way the soft jersey of her dress was stretched over her breasts. Breasts that seemed fuller, somehow…heavier.

She felt the alcohol creaming in her bloodstream, heating it. Making her feel different… oh, so different. Free…bold…daring.

Daring enough to sit there with the devastating homage to manhood that was Max Vasilikos, whose lidded eyes were resting on her, whose sensual smile was playing around his mouth. His long lashes were veiling but not concealing the expression in his deep, dark eyes. That thrill came again in her…electricity crackled along her nerve fibres. She was no longer the person she had been—she was someone else now. Someone new.

Someone a man like Max could desire?

Because why else was he sitting there so close, so intimately, his eyes holding hers as if by a silken thread that was drawing her towards him, closer and closer yet? Why else—unless he desired her?

Wonder and hope welled up in her. Was this truly happening? All those long, lost years when she'd been trapped in despising her body, her face…were they really over? Was it possible that she could now reach out and take what was surely every woman's right—could taste and enjoy the sensual pleasures of the flesh?

A memory pressed at her of her time at university, studying sports science, when all about her everyone had been pairing off, partying... and she had not dared. She'd felt excluded, forbidden from trying to join in. Had drawn back and hidden away, feeling herself unworthy—for who could want a woman like *her*? Men could only possibly want women like Chloe...who was the total opposite of herself.

I banished myself—did not dare to try and claim the place that every other woman was claiming.

But now—oh, now she *did* dare! She *did* dare to lean back into her end of the sofa, to relax and take a deep, easing breath.

And the absolute proof of her right to dare was the expression in Max Vasilikos's eyes now, as he twined his gaze with hers. The dim light cast shadows, created an atmosphere that was as heady as the liqueur she was sipping. She felt relaxed, languorous. And yet that low electric current was humming all the time, fuelling the charge that was building up in her, circuit by circuit.

Desire quickened in her veins. Desire made her eyelids heavy. Her breathing was shallow, her awareness of the sheer, raw physicality of Max becoming heightened…super-aware, ultra-aware.

I want this! I want what is to happen. I want it with all my being. To taste what I have denied myself so long…what I have never dared to take…

Yearning filled her, fusing throughout her being.

He moved first.

Wordlessly he placed his cognac glass on the table. Wordlessly he reached to remove her glass from her hand and do likewise. Wordlessly he curved his hand around the nape of her neck. Silently, his heavy-lidded eyes lambent upon her he drew her lithe, pliant body towards him.

And as his mouth closed over hers in the sweet heat of his kiss there was only one conscious thought left in her head.

If Max Vasilikos desires me, then I am desirable indeed!

And then all conscious thought fell from her. Now there was only sensation—sensation so strong, so overpowering, so arousing, so incredible, so blissful, so pleasurable, so *fantastic* that there was room for nothing else at all in her entire existence. His kiss was as skilled as it was consuming, unhurried—leisurely, even—as touch by touch, graze by graze, his mouth explored hers, slowly at first, skimming her lips, then deepening moment by expert moment, deepening until she was lost, yielding to what he was arousing in her, igniting in her, as each touch of his lips set new fires within her. Fires that he stoked, and stroked as his fingertips explored the nape of her neck, grazed the tender lobes of her ears, as his mouth moved to nuzzle at them softly, sweetly, arousingly.

She felt her breasts engorge and strain, and then a hand was cupping one, and a whole explosion of sensation ignited within her. A soft gasp sounded in her throat as he coaxed her cresting nipple to exquisite arousal. Her hand pressed against the hard-muscled wall of his chest, fingers splaying out, finding as if by instinct the shirt buttons, reaching between, within, slipping one and then another undone as if this were a skill that had been innate inside her all her life.

She heard him groan as her palm slid across the bare skin of his chest, slid down to where his belt snaked around his hips, eased along the rim of it. And he groaned again, his hand tightening on her breast, his mouth devouring hers now.

Excitement ripped through her, raw and intense. She pulled her mouth away, gazed at him, lips parted, eyes flaring, spearing her free hand into the hair that feathered at the base of his skull, shaping it with her fingers. There was an urgency in her now. A sense of power. She felt ripped, pumped, with adrenaline flowing in her, strong and purposeful. She knew what she wanted. *Who* she wanted.

A lioness seeking her mate…

His mouth curved into a smile. A smile of triumph. She knew it, gloried in it.

Their eyes twined together as they half lay upon the sofa that was suddenly much too small.

With a single fluid movement he got to his feet, scooping her up with him. She gave a cry that was half a gasp, for she knew just how much she weighed, even though it was muscled mass, not fat, but it didn't faze him in the slightest. As if she were a feather he carried her through to his bedroom, lowered her down on the bed. But he didn't come down beside her, remaining on his feet.

He wasn't idle, though. He was shrugging off his unbuttoned shirt, ripping the tie from him, ripping everything from him. Her eyes widened—how could they not?—and then, belatedly, she started to work off her own dress.

A hand stayed her.

'Oh, no,' growled Max. 'That's for *me* to do.'

He drew her back to her feet, utterly shameless in his own nakedness, his own rampant arousal. And she, because of that, was shameless too, standing there in front of him, fully clothed, her hands reaching up to her head, pulling off the hairclip so that her tousled locks fell with a single sensuous shake of her head, rippling down her back.

She heard him growl in satisfaction, saw his eyes flaring in the near darkness, for the only light came from the dim lamp in the lounge beyond. It was all the light they needed, and now he was stepping towards her, his hands catching at the hem of her dress, drawing up the soft jersey material in a slow, unstoppable movement until he'd eased it clear off her shoulders and freed her from it, casting it unwanted to a nearby chair. Now it was just her, with her hair rippling down her back, and the underwear she stood in.

But not for long.

Her own hands reached behind her back and she unhooked her bra deliberately, displaying herself, her eyes holding his all the time, her chin lifted, lips parted, knowing *exactly* what she was doing. Her breasts were freed, the bra discarded to the floor, and she stood there, showing her body to him as he was showing his to her.

His expression changed. 'My beautiful lioness...' he said, and his voice was low, deep, husky. His hand reached forward and the tips of his fingers simply grazed across her peaked nipples, so that they flowered even more, and a whisper of delight, of pleasure so exquisite, rippled through her so that she gasped and her head fell back, her long tousled hair brushing across the lower reaches of her arching spine.

He cupped her full, engorged breasts, heavy in his hands, and then his mouth found hers again, slowly, sensuously, with an intensity of arousal that she knew, with a kind of glory inside her, was the beginning of ultimate consummation.

She let him press her down upon the bed, let his body come over her, felt the crushing, arousing weight of him. He was kissing her still, one hand still enclosing a breast, the other now despatching the last remaining obstacle to his imminent possession. She lifted her hips as he discarded her panties and then she let his hand slide between her thighs, parting them for him. Whirls of pleasure rose within her, each one more intense than the last. A mist descended over her consciousness. She was no longer a thinking being—only a feeling one. Giving herself to the ultimate sensation.

He nestled himself within the apex of her body, and she felt with a mix of shock and exultation just how ready he was for this. How ready *she* was...

He took her hands, lifted them above her head so that the peaks of her breasts lifted too, and she gazed up at him. He smiled. Slow, intimate— possessive.

With an instinct older than time she felt her hips lift a little, straining towards him, yearning for his possession. His name was on her lips. An invitation—a plea. His smile deepened. And then, in a sudden fluid movement, he pulled away from her—only a fraction, but it was enough to cause alarm to flare in her eyes. Until she realised what he was doing—reaching into the drawer beside his bed...finding protection. *Her* protection.

She shut her eyes—there were things that even as a lioness she could not cope with! She heard him laugh, as if he realised that. A kiss nuzzled at the tip of her nose.

'Safe to peek now,' he said.

Amusement was in his voice, but it was only on the surface. Below was something deeper, and far more primal. She opened her eyes, looked deep into his, and even in the semi-darkness the naked desire there, the raw arousal, shocked her like electricity jolting through her body— her inflamed, aroused body.

For one long moment he gazed down at her. 'My lioness,' he murmured. 'My strong, beautiful lioness!'

And then, with a slow, deliberate tensing, he lowered himself to her as her thighs parted for him, as her hips lifted to his, as her body opened to his. Taking possession of her.

As she did of him.

There was tightness, but no resistance. She drew him into her, her body welcoming his, glorying in it, her delicate silken tissues gliding him in, sending a million nerve endings firing, shooting volley after volley of pleasure through her.

How could it be so good—so good to feel like this? How could this fullness be so incredible? This fusion, this melding of their flesh?

She dimly realised that for a moment he did not move, with supreme self-control, letting her body accommodate itself around him, letting her revel in the fullness of their fusion, letting her body reach the same level as his, poised at the brink.

Her hands were on his shoulders, braced against him, and his hands were bearing his weight, for he did not want to crush her. He wanted to see her face—a face that was raised to him in wonder, in beauty—in the moment before the ecstasy took her...took him...

And then, with the slightest shift in muscle, he moved, letting himself release.

He saw it happen in her face, saw her eyes distend, and then he was beyond everything but his own conflagration which swept up through him like a firestorm, burning him to ashes. Burning her with him.

She cried out in wonder, in amazement, in pleasure, and the sound of her cry shook him to his core. Her spine arched, her hips straining at him, nails clutching at his shoulders, head thrown back so that he could see the ecstasy that was in her face, the wonder and the joy. He felt her body thrash around him, pulsing with consummation, felt her thighs straining taut against his, and then his arms were around her, holding her, cradling her, keeping her safe within his embrace as her body burned.

And then slowly, oh-so-slowly, she slackened in his arms—slowly, oh-so-slowly, she stilled, her eyelids fluttering, her breath ragged, her skin dampened with a silken sheen. He held her tight against him, still half possessing her, then slackened away from her. He smoothed her hair, so fine and soft, and spoke to her in his native tongue. He knew not what he said. And she was like one who had gone beyond—gone far beyond, to a place she had never been before.

He held her while her taut muscles relaxed, released their tension, became soft and lax. She was letting him rock her gently, oh-so-gently, and he held her, still murmuring to her, as he brought her back slowly, carefully...oh-so-carefully.

He kissed her forehead, with scarcely any energy left in him to do so, and then a great lassitude swept through him. An exhaustion of the senses, of the passions. He turned her in his arms, her body still damp, her eyes still glazed, and kissed her bare shoulder, nestling her into him, holding her close and safe and warm against him.

'Sleep,' he said, his voice a murmur. 'Sleep now...'

He saw the ghost of a smile cross her mouth. It was all that she could manage and he asked for no more—not now. She had given all and taken all, and now they would rest, exhausted and complete, embraced by each other.

Sleep took them both.

CHAPTER NINE

ELLEN STIRRED. SHE was cradled against hard, warm muscle, and an arm lay heavily around her. She could feel Max's breathing, low and steady, feel his breath on the nape of her neck. As she came to wakefulness her own limbs felt heavy, tired, and there was an ache between her legs. Yet it was not pain. Oh, no, not pain...

A sense of wonder suffused her. Was it real to be lying here in the dim morning light, with Max's arms around her, holding her so closely? Could it possibly be real? But it was—oh, it *was*. That was the wonder of it—the miracle. That after all those long, miserable years of thinking herself repulsive, repellent, all the misery, the dreary self-torment, was over.

Gratitude flooded her. She knew why Max had done this, knew what his reasons were—to wean her away from clinging to the home she loved so much, that he could only see as her hiding place—but she didn't care. How could she care when his strong arms were warm around her? When her body had discovered the bliss he could arouse in her? No, whatever his motives, she could only be grateful for this wondrous, incredible gift that he had given her—the gift of knowing herself to be desirable.

It was gratitude that she gave voice to when Max awoke and made love to her again, bringing her once more to a peak of ecstasy that left her breathless with wonder. Then another appetite struck, and they wrapped themselves in voluminous bathrobes, padded through to the suite's dining area to partake of a large and filling breakfast.

She caught his hand, staying him. Her eyes huge. *'Thank you...'* she breathed.

He turned her hand in his, winding his fingers through hers, turning them towards him. Amusement danced in his eyes, but there was another expression there too.

'Oh, the pleasure was all mine—be very, *very* sure of that!'

He kissed her nose, lightly and humorously, squeezing her hand, his free hand brushing the loosened locks of her hair caressingly. She was gazing up at him wide-eyed, with that wonder in her expression that did strange things to him. There was wonder in him, too. He'd awakened her senses—but she had awakened in him senses he had not known he possessed.

Satisfaction—deep, consuming and very...well, very *satisfying*—creamed through him. Whatever his original motives for setting Ellen free from the chains she was bound with, he knew with absolute certainty that what had happened between them—what was still happening—was for quite different reasons. For reasons that had only to do with him being a man and Ellen being a woman, desiring him and being desired.

That is all we need. All I want.

He sat himself down opposite her, reaching for her glass and filling it with fresh orange juice from the jug on the table. His eyes rested on her, appreciating what he was seeing—her loose, tousled hair, the deep vee of her robe exposing the swell of her breasts, the softness in her face, in her eyes, the deep, sensuous glow of a woman who'd spent a night of passion in his arms.

He poured his own orange juice and drank it in

one draught, setting down the glass. She was sipping hers in a more genteel fashion, and her gaze was flickering to his, as if she wanted to feast on him but felt a touch of shyness yet. Hunger rattled in him—and not just for the croissants nestling in their napery. He helped himself to one, tearing it open with strong fingers. Then his eyes went back to hers, holding them.

'We need,' he announced, 'to get hold of your passport.'

Ellen started. She'd been in a daze, wanting only to let her eyes gaze across the table at him, to drink him in—the way his jaw was roughened right now, and how enticingly piratical the dark shadow of regrowth made him look, and how there was that glint in his eyes again that could melt her bones like water, and how the towelling robe he wore with such casual ease was so incredibly white against the gold tan of his smooth, half bared chest, and how his strong, lean forearms were reaching for that croissant with fingers that had stroked her body to shuddering ecstasy.

'What?' Her eyes widened in confusion.

'Your passport,' Max repeated. His expression

changed, become amused. 'So we can visit my eco-resort in the Caribbean. I told you over dinner last night that I needed to go out there.' Long lashes dipped over his dark eyes. 'Surely,' he said softly, 'you did not think that a single night with you would be enough—did you?'

He watched his words sink in. Words that he had already formed in his own head as soon as he'd awoken. A single night with this woman? No, not enough! Not anywhere *near* enough!

Across from him he saw her reaction—saw for the fraction of a second indecision hover in her eyes and then vanish.

Her face lit, and inside her head words were singing suddenly.

Go with him! Go with him while he wants you—because he does want you. Because this time is the most wonderful of your life so far. So seize it—seize it all. Take what you've never had before and wring from it every last drop. After all, why not?

Max Vasilikos had given her a gift she had never, never thought to possess—the gift of her own beauty. The gift of himself desiring her.

Wonder, joy and gladness filled her to the brim.

* * *

'There are no walls!' Ellen exclaimed as they walked into the room. It was situated in one of the cabanas that had already been constructed, at one end of the resort, and was cantilevered over a low, rocky bluff that jutted right out over a sheltered bay on the tiny islet.

'Just mosquito nets,' agreed Max. He strolled up to the missing outer wall, where an area of decking gave some outside space to meld interior and exterior seamlessly. 'Like it?' he asked as Ellen walked up to join him, resting her hands on the balustrade above the tumbling rocks.

A little wooden staircase to their left led down to the white sand beach a few metres below. An azure sea lapped lazily, beckoning to her with seductive allure.

She twisted her head to look at him. Made a face. 'Oh, no, it's awful—honestly, how could you bring me to such a place? I mean, there isn't a nightclub for miles, and there's no gourmet restaurant with a signature chef, and, I mean, there isn't even a *wall*, for heaven's sake!'

In the hours it had taken them to arrive here the very last remnants of her shyness and uncertainty in his company had vanished. Gone completely. Now she was at ease with him, daring to laugh with him, be confident with him, to tease him as she was doing now.

He kissed her to silence her and they both laughed into the kiss, and then Max tightened his hold and deepened his kiss. 'There is, however,' he told her, 'a bed—a very large, king-sized bed—and the mattress is very, *very* high spec… I promise you.'

It was, too, and suddenly all jet lag was gone, and energy and the fires of arousal leapt within her, dismissing all other thoughts.

'I wanted to swim in the sea,' was her last muffled cry as he swept her off to the bed.

'Later…' Max growled.

Afterwards, as they lay exhausted in each other's sated embrace, it came to him that for a woman who had only a handful of days ago regarded herself as completely repellent to the male race, she was, in fact, taking to this like a natural. As if she'd been born to be in his arms…

Ellen waded out of the water, feeling the heat of the sun on her body immediately, even through her sopping wet T-shirt. Her snorkel and mask dangled loose in her hand.

'Lunch?' asked Max, glancing at her and admiring the way the wet T-shirt material clung to her generous breasts. Desire stirred in him. Maybe they could wait for lunch for a while?

'Definitely,' agreed Ellen, dashing his hopes, or at least deferring them until a post-lunch siesta.

Ellen glanced fondly at him. The days had slipped by, one after another, each one glorious. They'd swum and snorkelled, sailed and kayaked, and Ellen had done a beginner's dive while Max, with years of experience, had gone for a serious deep water session.

She'd accompanied Max as he'd inspected the resort site, talking to his project manager, the architect and the work crew who came across from the main island, where they lived. It had been revealing to see him with his staff, because even the most junior of the work crew got a word of appreciation from him, and she'd been able to see they regarded him as a good boss.

That said a lot about a person...things she could admire, respect. No mere venal money-grubbing property developer was he—his values were those she could share and approve of.

'There are places in the world where new construction is fine—and places where it isn't,' Max was saying now as they relaxed, replete after dinner cooked over an open firepit, down on their little beach, leaning back against a rock with the water lapping gently a few metres away and overhead the tropical stars wheeling their slow arc across the midnight sky. 'Places where we should tread lightly on the land, as I'm trying to do here, or not tread at all—places where we should save and repair what is already there, conserve what earlier generations have built.'

She glanced at him, liking what she'd heard him say. 'Maybe being Greek helps—growing up amongst so much antiquity?'

But her words drew from him a glance that seemed, she felt, to admonish her.

'We cannot live in the past—it is not healthy to do so. Sometimes,' he said, 'we have to let go. Let go of the past and make a new future for ourselves! A new life.'

Ellen's eyes slipped away. Discomfort snagged in her, and she wished he had not said that. This was the first time he'd referred to the underlying reason he was in her life at all. Up till now there had been no mention of it—as if that troubled situation thousands of miles across the ocean did not exist. And certainly it had not intruded into what they had here.

Here, she knew—with a gratitude that in itself was revealing of how much she did not want to think of anything beyond this bliss—she could merely revel in what was happening. Day after day, just her and Max—wonderful, *wonderful* Max!—who'd transformed her, transformed her life, and to whom she would be grateful always! Walking barefoot on the sand, hand in hand beneath the sun, beneath the moon and stars. All cares and concerns far, far away.

But now he was reminding her of them. Making her think about them...making her face them once again. She didn't want to hear him say such things. He'd made no mention before—none at all—of what was for this brief space of time an ocean away. Nor did she want him to.

I don't want this time with him spoilt in any way at all. I don't want to think about Haughton, how desperate I am to keep it. Nor to be told that I should let it go...

But Max was speaking again, gazing up at the starry night sky.

'I remade *my* life,' he was saying. 'My mother's death forced me to do so. I wish so much she'd lived to see what I've achieved, but it was not to be.'

His gaze flicked back to her, trying to read her expression in the dim light. But he could not see it. And nor could he bring himself to tell her how struck he'd been by the house he wanted her to yield to him—how it had called to him immediately, arousing in him for the first time in his life an urge to cease his wandering, rootless lifestyle.

Instead he focussed on what he so wanted her to realise for herself. 'Do you not think,' he ventured carefully, weighing the impact of each word upon her, 'that your father's death is also a turning point for *you*? Allowing you to be free at last to do what you want with your life?' He chose the word 'allowing' specifically. 'Allowing you,' he finished, his eyes on her, 'to move on. To claim your own life for yourself?'

With a sweep of his hand he indicated the whole

expanse of the beach, the starry tropical sky, the lap of the gentle waves.

'It's a good life, isn't it?' he said softly. 'Here—and everywhere! The whole world lies before you, Ellen, and now you know how beautiful you are, how desirable, what is stopping you from walking out into that world? Living your life. *Your* life, Ellen—unfettered and untrammelled. Not trapped in an unhappy past.'

She let him speak. She knew why he was saying it—knew it was because he wanted her to stop fighting him, stop clinging to Haughton. Knew that he truly believed it would be for her own good. But she could make no reply. Inside her, like a festering wound, was all the bitterness she felt about what Pauline's marriage to her father had done, and it could not be so easily lanced.

I don't want to think about them—what they did to my father, to me—not while I'm here, having this precious time with Max. I don't want to tell him what they're like, how vicious and ruthless they are—greedy for everything they can get their hands on. I don't want this idyll with Max spoilt.

So she looked away, giving a slow shake of her head, closing her eyes momentarily. Shutting out what he was telling her. Then she felt his hand on her arm, not pressing firmly, almost as a message to her.

'Think about what I've said…' His voice was low, compelling. 'That's all I ask for now.'

He paused, instinctively knowing that he must say no more now, that she must ponder his words, let them soak into her. Make sense to her.

He shifted his position, hooking his arms loosely around his splayed bent knees. 'So,' he said, his tone quite different now, 'what shall we do tomorrow? How about if we take the catamaran out?'

Gratefully, Ellen followed his lead. This was the Max she wanted. Carefree and easy-going. Revelling in the days and nights they spent here.

And she was grateful, too, the next day—to experience the thrill and the speed of skimming over the azure swell as she clung to the tarpaulin between the twin hulls of the wind-hungry vessel, with Max commandingly at the helm.

'Enjoying it?' he shouted to her over the rush of wind.

'Fantastic!' she yelled back, and then gave a cry, snatching more tightly at the tarpaulin, as with a careless answering laugh Max spun the helm, heading right into the wind, and the catamaran tacked with a lift of one hull before coming about again.

Exhilaration filled her as he headed downwind back to shore. With easy strength she helped him haul the vessel up on to the beach, then flopped down on the hot sand.

Max lowered himself beside her. Her eyes were shining, her face alight. There was sand in her hair, and it was windblown and tangled. A memory of how Tyla had hated getting her hair in a mess sifted through him—how she'd fussed endlessly about her appearance, wanting him and every other man to admire her constantly. Desire her.

His eyes softened. Ellen—his own beautiful lioness—was fit and fabulous. She'd believed no man could desire her, and even now that he had convinced her how very, very wrong that misconception had been, so that she now finally accepted the truth of her own appeal, there was still no trace of the fussing and self-absorption that Tyla had indulged in endlessly.

How easy that makes her to be with—she accepts my desire for her as naturally as breathing now, returns it with an ardour that takes my breath away!

And it was much more than simply the time she spent in his arms, breathtaking though that was. It was her enthusiasm, her sheer enjoyment of everything—from food, to sunbathing, to swimming, to gazing up at the stars—everything they did together.

I like being with her. I like her company—I like her thoughts and views and opinions. I like it that she likes this simple place and that she does not yearn for bright lights and sophisticated glamour. I like her laughter and her smiles.

She was smiling now—smiling right up at him as he loomed over her.

'Good fun?' He grinned, and she laughed again exuberantly. 'You can sail her tomorrow,' he promised, and then busied himself with kissing her.

From kissing her it was an easy progression to sweeping her up into his arms and carrying her up to their open-air room, making use, yet again, of the very large bed.

His last conscious thought, barely forming in his head, was just how good it was to make love with Ellen—how very, *very* good. And then there was no more thought, no more conscious awareness of anything at all, only rich, sating fulfilment.

Max's hand was resting lazily over Ellen's warm, sand-speckled thigh as they lay in partial shade on their little beach, having breakfasted on their terrace after an early-morning workout at the open-air gym in what would shortly be the reception and central services area of the resort. They were sunning themselves, waiting for enough wind to rise so they could take out the catamaran.

It was their penultimate day there, and Ellen was only too conscious of a sense of deep, aching reluctance for this blissful, wondrous time to end. She could feel a little tug on her insides—a sense of yearning for this time not to be over, not to be done with. She glanced over the sparkling azure water to the curve of the tiny bay edged with vivid glossy foliage. The fronded roofing of their wooden cabana was barely visible, blending into the verdant greenery.

She gave a low, regretful sigh. These past days—one slipping effortlessly into the next, so that she'd all but lost count of them—had been so wonderful. So idyllic. They had been cocooned on this lush tropical island, living as close to nature as they could. Away from all the rest of the world, away from all its problems and difficulties.

A little Eden—just for the two of us. And I was Eve—woman new-made. Discovering for the first time just how joyous being a woman can be.

New-made, indeed—and from Adam's rib. A smile tugged whimsically at her mouth.

Max made me—he made me a woman, sensual and passionate.

Oh, he'd done it for his own purposes, his own ends—she had no illusions about that. He had been perfectly open about wanting her to discover what life could be like beyond what she knew he saw as the prison of her childhood home. The place that had trapped her in misery, in the past, in her bitter feud with Pauline and Chloe. But she didn't care. How could she? His motives could never detract from the effect his liberation had had on her. The wondrous, glorious gift he had given her!

The gift of his own desire for her.

And hers for him.

Her eyes went to him now with familiar pleasure as he lay beside her on the sand, dark glasses shading his eyes so that she did not know if he was dozing or awake.

It was the latter. 'Why the sigh?' he asked, turning his head towards her.

'Oh, I guess it's just that I… Well… This time tomorrow we'll be heading back to London.'

She felt his gaze on her through the opaque lenses. 'You've enjoyed it here?'

There was a little choke in her voice. 'Of *course* I have! It's been idyllic.' It was all she could manage to say.

'Yes,' he agreed, 'it's certainly been that.'

His hand moved a fraction on her thigh, and he turned his head away to look up into the sky. She could hear a pause in his silence. Then he spoke.

'Tell me…'

His voice was different—almost, she thought, speculative.

'What do you think about Arizona?'

She frowned in surprise. 'Arizona?'

'Yes. Or actually it might be Utah. I'll have to check.' He turned his head towards her again, pushing his dark glasses up on to his head. 'Ever heard of Roarke National Park?'

She shook her head, still frowning slightly.

'Well,' Max continued, 'it's not as well-known as the more famous National Parks in the American West, such as Zion and Bryce—let alone the Grand Canyon. But, anyway, the lodge there is hosting a seminar on sustainable tourist development which I've a fancy to go to.'

He paused again, his eyes suddenly unreadable.

'So what do you say? Shall we head there next? We can fly from Miami. Once the seminar's done we could add a few days' hiking, maybe. Pick up boots and kit when we're there. Does it appeal?'

She was silent. Then suddenly she propelled herself up on her elbow, looking down at Max. '*Yes!* Oh, yes.'

In an instant her heart was singing, her mood soaring into the stratosphere. More time with Max—oh, yes, more time!

A grin split his face. 'Great,' he said.

He reached up a hand to her nape, drawing her mouth down to his, letting her hair fall like a veil around them. Satisfaction filled him. And a sense of triumph. Another new place, another new experience for Ellen to savour—to tempt her to stay out in the wonderful world that could be hers if she left her past behind her.

And, best of all, another stretch of time to enjoy all that she bestowed upon him.

His kiss deepened, and soon all thoughts of taking the catamaran out that morning faded completely.

CHAPTER TEN

ROARKE NATIONAL PARK proved to be an experience ideally suited to Ellen. She loved it—loved the wild beauty of the American West, loved even more experiencing it with Max.

They flew in to Salt Lake City, then drove down through the increasing grandeur of the landscape as it rose in a vast stone flight of inclined steps from the south. The park itself was still relatively quiet at this early time in the season, with parts of it still closed by snow, but in the sheltered canyon it was warmer, and the sunlit orange sandstone rock was a vivid contrast with the deep blue of the sky and the dark green of the pines.

The timber-built lodge fitted into its remote setting perfectly, blending into the landscape, a tribute in itself to the kind of design that worked best in places where nature was pre-eminent. And Ellen found the seminar fascinating—as fascinating as learning about the geology and geography of the park and the wider landscape beyond. Already she was planning a field trip here, making appropriate notes with which to broach the project with her headmistress on her return.

She made no mention of that to Max, however. She did not want to trigger another attempt by him to persuade her to abandon what he was so convinced were the confines of her life at Haughton. She did not want that upset. Wanted only to enjoy this time with him to the hilt.

And enjoy it she did.

As he'd promised, after the seminar they kitted themselves up with hiking gear and took to the trails that were open at that time of year.

'Boy…' she breathed as they reached the summit of one trail that had ascended up out of the canyon and on to a rocky plateau where the chill wind seemed only cooling after the heat generated by their hard-pushed muscles. 'You don't need a gym at this place, do you?'

Max gave a laugh, leaning back on a rock to take a long draught of water from the flask that hung around his neck—an absolute necessity for hiking, as they'd been firmly instructed by the rangers—and she did likewise.

'No, indeed,' he agreed. 'We're going to feel it in our legs tomorrow, though, I suspect. But it's worth it ten times over.'

'Oh, yes.' She nodded, her eyes sweeping out over the grandeur of the wilderness that stretched as far as the eye could see and much further still. Her gaze came back to Max. 'Thank you,' she said.

He smiled, warm and affectionate. 'I knew this was a good idea,' he said. He lowered his backpack to the ground. 'Right, that hike's made me starving—time for lunch.'

They settled themselves on a sun-warmed rock in the lee of a boulder that sheltered them from the keening wind and companionably started on the packed lunch prepared for them. Ellen lifted her face to the sun. Happiness filled her. Complete and absolute happiness.

Her eyes went to Max.

You...you make me happy. Being with you makes me happy. Whether we're making love or sitting like this, side by side in the silence and the grandeur of nature's gift to us. It's being with you that makes me happy.

Yet even as the thoughts filled her head their

corollary came. If being with Max made her happy, what would being *without* him make her?

For being without him was what awaited her. It had to—there could be no escape from that. In days they would be heading back to England.

And even if it were not mere days...even if it were weeks...even months...at some point I would have to be without him.

Shadows clouded her mind and through the shadows words pierced her. Pierced her with painful knowledge.

The longer I am with him, the harder being without him will be.

There was a little cry inside her head as the piercing knowledge came. Instinctively she sought to shield herself. To hold up a guard against the thought that must come next but which she would not permit. Dared not permit.

Fiercely she fought back.

Enjoy only this! Enjoy this for what it is and don't ask for more.

Yet even as she adjured herself to be cautious she knew with sudden certainty that it was already too late for caution. Awareness opened out within her like a physical sensation, and the

words that went with it took form in her consciousness—loud and unstoppable.

Am I falling in love with him?

She pulled her mind away, tried to silence the
words. Sought urgently to counter them. To deny
them. No—*no*—she *wasn't* falling in love with
Max. She was only *thinking* she was!

And it was obvious—wasn't it? Max was the
first man in her life...the only man to have made
love to her, embraced her, kissed her, spent time
with her. It was obvious that she should fancy
herself falling in love with him! What female
wouldn't fancy herself falling in love with him
when he was so incredibly attractive, so devastating, from his deep, dark eyes and his curving
smile to his strong, lean body?

That was all it was—just a natural and obvious
reaction. It was only that, nothing more—it was
nothing real...just her imagination.

Beside her, Max was packing away his now
empty lunch box and fishing out his phone.

'Selfie time,' he announced, hooking one arm
around her while holding out his phone ahead
of them. 'Big smile!' he instructed, and set off

a flurry of shots of them both. 'There,' he said, showing her the images.

Ellen smiled, but she could feel a pang inside all the same. A sudden sense of impending loss.

This is all that's going to be left of my time with him—photos and memories.

She took a steadying breath. Well, she would deal with that when she had to. Right now, as Max slipped his phone away and got to his feet, hefting his backpack on to his broad shoulders again, she would make the most of this time with him. So she got up too, and set off after him on the descent.

More hiking, cycling along the paved valley trails and even horse riding—with Ellen discovering the novelty of a Western saddle—comprised their days, and dining at the lodge in rustic comfort passed their evenings. Roaring log fires in the lounge and no TV or other electronic distractions all added to the ambience and mood. Yet all the same the days passed, one by one and ineluctably, taking them nearer to their return to the UK.

Ellen's mood, as they finally headed north to pick up their flight from Salt Lake City, became increasingly sombre as mile after long mile ate up this last time of being with the man who had so utterly transformed her.

Inside as well as outwardly.

An ache caught at her. Soon they would be parting. One plane journey away and she would be heading back to Haughton, and he—well, he would be heading to whatever was next on his busy schedule. This time tomorrow he would be gone from her life.

A silent cry went up inside her. And a savage admonition.

You went into this with your eyes open. You knew why he was doing it, what his reasons were—so don't bewail it. Think of it as...as therapy!

She shut her eyes, blocking the sight of him from herself. There would be other men in her life now. He had made that possible. Made her see herself as desirable, as beautiful. That was the gift he'd given her, even if he'd given it to her for reasons of his own. From now on she knew that men would desire her—

But even as she told herself that she could hear that voice cry out again in silent anguish.

But what man could I desire after Max? What man could ever compare to him? Impossible— just impossible! No one could ever melt me with a single glance, could make love to me as he does, could set the fires racing through my veins as he can! No one! No one else ever will.

A shiver went through her, as if she had stirred ghosts from a future that had not yet happened but was waiting to happen. A future without Max Vasilikos in it. An empty future.

No, she mustn't think like that. A future without Max in it would not be empty. Could not be—not while she had to fight for her beloved home, keep it as long as she possibly could, safe from those who wanted to take it from her. Including Max.

Her face shadowed. Here, on the far side of the Atlantic, she had been able to forget that it was he who wanted to oust her—for her own good, as he believed—but that bitter truth was not something she must ever forget.

And it was a truth that loomed larger with every hour on the plane as they flew back to the UK.

Her mood had darkened as they flew into the night, and she had slept only patchily and uncomfortably. She knew she had a sombre air about her as they arrived at Heathrow in the bleak early hours of the morning. She was facing the end of her time with Max and the resumption of her battle for her home.

After the tropical heat of the Caribbean, and the crisp, clean air of the American west, the wet spring weather of the UK was uninviting and drear as a chauffeured car drove them into London through the rush hour traffic.

Ellen sat huddled into a corner, groggy from the red-eye flight, and Max let her be, busying himself with catching up on his emails on his laptop. Thoughts were racing across his mind.

As they stepped out on to the pavement outside the hotel he shivered extravagantly. 'It's freezing!' he exclaimed. He ushered her inside the hotel, and as they reached the warmth of the lobby said, 'Thank goodness the Gulf is our next destination!'

He didn't notice Ellen's sudden start at his words, only guided her into the elevator. Back in his suite, he elaborated, watching as room service departed after setting breakfast out for them.

'I've just had confirmation via email that my

appointment with the business adviser to the Sheikh there is the day after tomorrow. It will be a bit of a rush, but we can fly out tomorrow. You can cope with that, can't you?' He smiled. 'We'll stay on—go camping in the Arabian desert. Stargazing, camel rides, dune-bashing—you'll love it.' Then his expression changed. 'What is it?' he asked.

Concern was in his voice. Ellen was just looking at him in consternation.

'Max... Max, I can't,' she said.

He frowned. 'You've still got a while before your next term starts,' he said.

She shook her head. Her expression had not changed. 'It's not that,' she said.

'Then what is it?' he demanded.

There was an edge in his voice he could not suppress. Emotion was starting up inside him. An emotion he did not want to feel, but that was happening all the same. Why was she hesitating like this? Making objections? Didn't she *want* to come out to the Gulf with him?

Because I certainly want her to come with me. I don't want to let her go—not yet. Definitely not yet.

Emotion swirled within him. He was certain—two hundred per cent certain—that he had no desire whatsoever to part company with Ellen now. That conviction had been growing with every passing day they'd spent together, and had come to a head on their overnight flight, when he'd realised he did not want their time together to end yet.

She'd been a revelation to him—a total revelation. Not just in her new-found physical beauty, which had knocked him for six from the moment she'd walked out looking so incredibly fantastic in that Edwardian ballgown, but ever since… And, no, not just in that respect. But more—oh, *much* more!

I like being with her. She's good company. Fun, intelligent, with a great sense of humour. She's easy-going, undemanding. She enjoys everything, is good-tempered, isn't self-obsessed or demanding of my attention—though I'm more than happy to lavish it on her because I so enjoy being with her.

The litany ran on in his head, concluding with the most obvious reason of all. In bed, he and she set off fireworks!

Ardent, passionate, sensual, sensitive, affectionate...

The litany set off again. And was cut brutally short as she shook her head again. He saw emotion flash across her face, then vanish. There was something different about her suddenly. Something that reminded him, with a sudden flicker of concern, an inward frown, of the way she'd looked when he'd first gone to look over Haughton and succumbed to its charms. As if she were locked inside herself. Shutting out the world. Shutting *him* out.

And he didn't want that. He didn't want it at all.

OK, he allowed, trying to rationalise her reaction, so she was jet-lagged. Flying the red-eye was never a fun experience. But her wavering was more than just sleep deprivation and grogginess. His thoughts raced on swiftly. Was it because although *he* was two hundred per cent sure he had no desire to call it quits between them, *she* might not realise that? Was she feeling uncertain about him? About what they had between them?

He took her hand in his, squeezed it tight. Time to reassure her.

'Ellen—we are *good* together. Never doubt that.

So let's go on making the most of it until your term starts. Don't cut this short unnecessarily—come with me to the Gulf! I want to show you as much of the world as I can. I want—'

But she tugged her hand free, stepping a pace away from him, her face working. Emotions were swilling within her—a turbulent mix. All the way back on the flight it had been worsening with the knowledge that her time with Max was ending. And it *must* end. That was the blunt truth of it. She would be back at school, and Max would either be pressing ahead with his proposed purchase of her home—although Pauline would have to start legal proceedings against her to force a sale—or else he would be backing off and leaving Haughton alone.

Whichever he did, her time with him would have ended. And while part of her—the part that had her heart leaping at the thought of what his words meant—was saying, *Go with him now—take these last few days with him!* she could not let herself listen to it. A few more days and then she would be back here again, just as she was now, and their time together would be over.

Better for it to be over now. Because the longer

you are with him, each and every day, the worse it will be for you when it's finally over. The more you will fear that you're falling in love with him—which you must not do. You must not!

Because whether she was falling in love with him, or whether it was just an obvious reaction to her first romance, it was going to hurt, doing without Max—it was hurting already…had been hurting all the way across the Atlantic…this prospect of her time with Max running out, reaching its close.

I'm going to have to do without him. I'm going to have to go home, back to my life, and keep fighting for Haughton to the bitter end.

So she had to crush down the rush of joy that came from the knowledge that Max wanted to spend more time with her.

She sought for the right words to say to him. 'Max, I can never thank you enough for what you've done for me. *Never!*' Emotion filled her voice, though it was low and strained. 'You've given me a gift I never thought to have—and this time with you has been…*miraculous.* I'll always be grateful to you—'

He cut across her. 'I don't want your gratitude!

I want you to come to the Gulf with me, make the most of our time now, before your term starts again. It's not too much to ask of you, is it?'

His tone was persuasive, compelling, but there was an edge to it as well. Didn't she *want* to be with him for longer? That bite of emotion came again, and with it another spiralling upwards of frustration.

She was staring across at him, her hands lifted as if—damn it—as if she were holding him at bay. Ellen was holding him off—

Emotion bit in him again, more painful this time.

'Max—it isn't that. It's…it's just that it'll only be postponing the time when I have to get back to Haughton. And it seems to me that it might as well happen now, rather than in a few days' time, when I'll just be right back here, facing the same situation. I *have* to go back to Haughton. And it isn't just because term is starting, it's because it's where I *want* to be—'

She broke off. Echoing bleakly in her head were the unspoken words—*while I still have it.*

But that was too painful even to think—too painful to say to the man who was trying to take it from her. Even though she knew that if it was not him who wanted to buy it at some point someone else would, and Pauline and Chloe would force the sale through, and she would lose the place she held so dear to her. The place where all her happiness was centred.

Yet even as the clutch of emotion that always came when she thought of Haughton gripped her, so did another.

All my happiness? And what of the happiness I've had with Max? What of that?

But her mind sheered away. Whatever happiness she'd had with Max, it was never, ever going to be anything other than temporary. How could it be otherwise? He'd transformed her into a woman who could finally indulge in her own sensuality—a gift she would always be grateful for, just as she'd told him. But for him…? Well, she was just a…a novelty, maybe, made all the more intriguing by the revelation of her desirability for him. Whatever her appeal for him, she had to accept that she was no more than a good companion, in bed and out, while they were together.

'We're good together,' he'd said, and it was true.

But it did not make it anything more.

Time for me to go home.

She shook her head, her expression anguished now. 'I just want to go home, Max,' she said. 'It's all I want to do.'

Even as she spoke she could feel that anguish spearing her. Yes, she wanted to go home—to be there while she still could, before it was torn from her—but it was not all she wanted. She wanted Max—oh, how she wanted him, to be with him—but even if she stayed now it would only be putting off what must be the inevitable end, only be making it worse for herself. So best for her to go now—go now and have precious time at the home that she could only lose in the end.

He saw her expression and hated seeing it. Hated hearing her say what she had said. Telling him she didn't want to be with him—wanted instead to return to the place he was trying to free her from. Frustration boiled up in him— more than frustration. It was an emotion he did not want to name, *could* not name. It boiled over. He stepped towards her, closed his hands around her arms, fastening her to him.

'Ellen, don't do this. Your obsession with

Haughton isn't healthy. It's poisoning you. Chaining you to a life you should not be living!'

His voice was urgent, his expression burning. Here they were, not an hour back in the UK, and she was already reverting to what she'd been like when he'd first known her. He had to stop that—right now! He had to make her see what she was doing to herself. Had to convince her, finally, that she *must* set herself free from her self-imposed chains. Chains that were as constraining and as deadly as those of her belief that she lacked beauty or desirability had been.

He took a shuddering breath, surged on with what he *must* say to her now to set her free.

Free to seize life with both hands. Free to take all it offers. Free to be with me—

Words were pouring from him. He could not stop them. He'd tried to be gentle on her during their time together, tried to ease her into seeing how she had to let the past go, not cling to it, had to move forward with her life, not stay trapped in the mesh of resentment she so obviously felt about her father's remarriage, unable to free herself of it. He had to make her see that now—in all its stark, unvarnished truth—or she'd just go right back into it all again. And be lost...

Lost to *him*...

An even greater urgency fuelled his words. 'You call it home—but it's a tomb, Ellen. *Your* tomb. Don't you see? You've buried yourself in it, clung to it, and you go on clinging to it because you can use it as a weapon against Pauline, who dared to marry your doting father and give him a second chance of happiness—'

A cry broke from her but he did not stop. Could not stop.

Frustration surged in him, boiling up out of the long, sleep-depriving red-eye flight that had taken them from their passion-filled carefree travels together to land them back here.

Ellen—*his* Ellen—whom he'd freed from her self-imposed mental prison of thinking herself unlovely and undesirable, was now determined to go straight back to the destructive life he'd released her from. He couldn't bear to let it happen. He had to make her see what she was doing to herself, consumed by bitterness as she was. It was a bitterness that was destroying her. Changing her from the wonderful, carefree, passionate woman she'd been when she was with him. Changing her back into the embittered, resentful, anger-obsessed person he'd first encountered.

He couldn't let that happen. He couldn't!

He plunged on. 'Ellen—look at yourself. You've let your anger and resentment eat into you. For years and years. You never gave Pauline and Chloe a chance—you never wanted them to be part of your family. You were fixated on your father—understandably, because of the loss of your mother—but now you've become obsessed with punishing them by hanging on to Haughton.'

She thrust him away, lurching backwards. Her eyes were wide and distended. Emotion battered at her. Stress, weariness and anger rushed up in her.

'It's my *home*, Max! Why *should* I sell it so that someone like you can turn it into a hotel? Or sell it on to some oligarch or sheikh who'll only set foot it in once a year, if that!'

He shook his head vigorously. 'That *isn't* what I want to do with Haughton. What I want is—'

She didn't let him finish. Dear God, why was he choosing now, of all times, to lay into her again? Why couldn't he just leave her alone? Stop going on and on about it?

'I don't *care* what you want! I don't care because I will fight you to the last—fight Pauline and Chloe to the last. Haughton is my home, and all I want—*all* I want—is to live there in peace!'

Max's hand slashed through the air. Exasperation and anger and emotions that were far more powerful than both of them fuelled his outburst. 'Then do it! Just damn well *do* it! Stop your venomous, vengeful feud with your stepmother, which is twisting you and poisoning you, and buy them out.'

He saw her freeze, his words stopping her in her tracks.

'Buy them out...' It was not a question, not a statement. Merely an echo. Her face was blank—quite blank.

He took a heavy breath. 'Yes, buy them out. If that is how you feel, Ellen, then simply buy their share from them so they can make a new life for themselves somewhere miles away from you, since I'm sure they feel the same way themselves. And then there'll finally be an end to this sorry saga. God knows I've tried to show you how good your life can be, but while you cling to your vendetta, keep punishing Pauline and Chloe, the poison is destroying you.'

He shook his head. He was beating it against a brick wall, he could see. He turned away, pouring himself a cup of coffee and knocking it back, as if to restore energy levels that were suddenly drained dry. Could *nothing* make her see what she was doing to herself?

There was the lightest touch on his arm. Ellen was there, drawing his attention. He put down the drained cup and turned.

There was something strange in her expression—something he'd never seen before. And it chilled him to the core.

Her voice, when she spoke was thin…thin like a needle. 'You said I should buy out Pauline and Chloe's share of Haughton…' Something flared in her eyes like a black flame. *'What with?'* The words were spat at him.

Exasperation lashed from him. 'Ellen, don't be melodramatic,' he said crushingly. 'You could easily buy them out if you wanted. Pauline told me that you'd inherited everything else your father left—his stocks, his shares, all his other assets. She told me herself he was a very wealthy man.'

He saw her face whiten like a bone. Bleach-white. The hand on his sleeve seemed to spasm. But when she spoke her voice was very calm. Too calm.

'Let me tell you something, Max.'

Her hand dropped like a dead weight from his arm. There was something odd about the way she was looking at him. Something that made him think of a mortally wounded animal.

'Do you remember the night of that Edwardian ball? The jeweller who arrived with all that jewellery for hire? Do you remember I chose the rubies immediately?'

There was something wrong with her voice too, and it made Max frown.

'It was not just because they went with my gown. It was because—'

And now there was definitely something wrong with her voice—with her eyes—with her white face and stiffened body.

'Because they once belonged to my mother. I recognised them instantly—especially the ring. It was her engagement ring. And it was my great-grandmother's before that—as was the rest of the parure. My mother liked the old-fashioned setting. But Pauline did not.'

And now Ellen's eyes had a different expression in them—one that Max found was causing the blood in his veins to freeze.

'So she sold it. She sold a great deal of my mother's jewellery, only keeping what she liked. Or what Chloe liked. They both like pearls, as it happens, in particular. The double pearl necklace Pauline was wearing when you came to lunch was my father's tenth anniversary present to my mother, and the pearl bracelet Chloe wore was given to me by my parents for my thirteenth birthday. Chloe helped herself to it—said it was wasted on me. Wasted on me because I was nothing but a clumsy great elephant, an ugly lump, totally *gross*. And she never, ever missed an opportunity to remind me of that! Wherever and whenever. She made me a laughing stock at school for it, and has gone on laughing ever since—she's mocked me mercilessly ever since her mother got her claws into my poor, hapless father!'

Max saw her take a breath—just a light, short

breath—before she plunged on. There was still the same chilling light in her eyes, in her voice.

'When Pauline married my father he was, indeed, a very wealthy man. It was his main attraction for her, his money—she just loved spending it. And so she spent and she spent and she *spent*! She spent it all. *All* of it! She spent it on endless holidays to expensive places—spent a fortune on interior designers both at Haughton and for the flat in Mayfair she insisted on. And she spent it on couture clothes for herself and Chloe, and on flash cars that were renewed every year, and more and more jewellery for themselves, and endless parties and living the high life at my father's expense.

'She burned through the lot. He sold everything in the end—all his stocks and shares, and some of the most valuable paintings. He cashed in all his funds and his life insurance, just to keep her in the luxury she demanded for herself. He died with almost nothing except Haughton—and he left two-thirds of that to Pauline and Chloe. Pauline made sure of that when he had to make a new will once he'd remarried. Made very, *very* sure!

'So you see, Max—' there was a twisting in her

voice now, like the wire of a garrotte '—there is absolutely *nothing* left of my father's wealth except what Haughton represents, so it would be hard for me to buy out Pauline and Chloe on my teacher's salary. That goes on paying for groceries and council tax and utility bills—and for my stepmother and stepsister's essential expenses. Like having their hair done. Their little jaunts abroad, of course, are paid for by systematically selling off the antiques and paintings left in the house.'

Her voice changed again, becoming mocking in its viciousness.

'To be fair to them, that's how I've decided I'm going to pay for the clothes I bought here in London. After all, why *shouldn't* I get just a fraction—a tiny, minute, minuscule fraction— of what my father's wife has taken? And by the same token, Max...'

The pitch of her voice chilled his blood once more, and the venom in her eyes was toxic.

'Why shouldn't I be just a tiny, teeny bit...*reluctant*...to let that pair of blood-sucking vampires sell my parents' home out from under my feet? *Why damn well shouldn't I?* Because it's all

I've got left. They've taken everything else—everything! They bled my father dry and made his life hell—*and* mine! And I will loathe their guts for it till my dying day.'

A shuddering breath escaped her, as if she were at the end of all her strength.

'So now, if you don't mind, Max, I'm going to go back to the place where I was born and raised, where I was once entirely happy until those...*vultures*...invaded it. The home I so fondly thought would one day be mine to raise my own family in, where I'd live out my days, but which is now going to be torn from me by my grasping, greedy, *vile* stepmother and stepsister, because it's the only thing left they can take. And I'm going to make the most of it—the *very* most of it—until the law courts, or the bailiffs, or your security guards or whatever it damn well takes drive me out of it.'

Her face contorted. She whirled around, seizing up her suitcase. He watched her stalk across the room, yank open the door, slam it shut behind her. Watched her while he stood motionless.

Quite, quite motionless.

CHAPTER ELEVEN

HAUGHTON WAS BATHED in watery sunlight, turning the house and gardens to pale silver, but as she stepped inside misery filled Ellen to the brim—for her father's ruin, her stepmother's avarice, for her angry parting with Max, for parting with him at all.

And for the loss of her home, which must come—now, or later, come it must.

As she went into the kitchen she could feel a dull, dread awareness forcing itself into her consciousness. A new, bitter truth pushing itself in front of her.

I can't go on like this. I just can't—not any longer.

Stark and brutal, the words incised themselves into her consciousness. She felt a pit of cold, icy water in her insides, a knot of dread and resolve. She had to face it—accept it. She could not stay locked in her vicious, destructive battle with Pauline and Chloe. It was a battle she could not win in the end. A battle that was indeed twisting her, deforming her.

I can't stop them taking it from me. I can't stop them and I can't go on the way I have been. So all I can do is give in. Give up. Give up my home.

More words echoed in her head, stinging even more painfully. Max calling this house a tomb. *Her* tomb. She felt her hands clench as if in desperate denial. But his accusation stabbed again. Forcing her to face what he had launched at her. Forcing her to face another truth as well.

I've changed. Max has changed me—changed not just my outer appearance but what is inside as well. I'm not the same person any more. Being with him, seeing the world with him, has changed me. He's opened my eyes to the world beyond here, given me the means to make the most of it, to stride through it with confidence and assurance.

I won't have him and I won't have Haughton—but I will have myself. And that must be enough. It must be enough because it is all that I can have now.

She knew it, accepted it—had no choice but to accept it.

But it was with a heavy heart and a sick feeling of dread and painful anguish that she went to make the phone call she knew she must make.

Max sat with an expression of polite interest on his face, as his meeting with the Sheikh's development minister proceeded. The meeting was going well, mutual benefits from his proposal were being agreed, relations were all extremely cordial and everyone all around was very pleased.

But Max's thoughts were far, far away, burningly consumed by a project that was small fry compared to the one being set up here, but ultimately far more important to him. One that was crucial to his future. His UK head of legal affairs had phoned him just as he'd arrived for his meeting and Max had mentally punched the air with relief.

The meeting finally over, with an entirely satisfactory conclusion, Max walked out to his waiting car. The heat of the Persian Gulf engulfed him. So did spearing emotion.

Ellen should be here. She should be at the hotel,

*by the pool. I'd join her and then enjoy a sund-
owner as the day cooled, looking forward to dinner together followed by an early night.*

*Then tomorrow we'd explore the souks of the
old city, with the scent of a thousand spices and
the fragrance of frankincense everywhere we
went, with gold glinting from a hundred stalls!
We'd cruise along the coast at sunset in a* dhow,
*watching the sun set over the city like a ball of
crimson flame.*

*The next day we'd drive into the desert, camp
out in the Empty Quarter, sleep under the stars
burning holes in heaven's floor...*

He tore his mind away. He must not indulge in
such wishful thinking. He must only look to the
future now—must get back to his hotel, phone
London, get matters expedited, concluded with
all possible haste. No delays could be tolerated.
The rest of his life depended on it.

Ellen glanced at her stopwatch, lifted her whistle
to her lips and blew sharply to call full time on
the match that was taking place on the pitch in
front of her. She shivered. A cold wind was blow-
ing, seemingly straight off the tundra hundreds

of miles to the north—the Canadian spring was later to arrive than the English one.

But she was grateful that her headmistress had looked to her to accompany the school's lacrosse team's visit to a school in Ontario at short notice when a fellow games teacher had had to pull out. Even more grateful for the invitation she had just received from the principal here—to spend the summer semester as an exchange teacher.

New horizons, a new life—Max would approve.

She sheered her mind away. *No—don't think of Max. Don't think of anything to do with him.* He was gone, out of her life now—gone from everything that had ever been anything to do with her. Except... She felt emotion twist inside her like a spasm, except from the one place on earth she had sought so desperately to keep—the place that a single phone call to her solicitor had severed from her for ever.

Maybe here, as she forged a new life for herself, she might start to forget the home she had lost. Maybe here, in the years to come, she might forget the man who had given her more than she had ever thought to have—who now possessed what she had feared so much to lose. Maybe. But she could not believe it. Because there was only one place on earth she wanted to call home. Only one man on earth she wanted to share it with.

Max! Oh, Max, why am I missing you so much? Why do I want only to rush back to you? To go with you wherever in the world you go, for however long you want me? Why do my dreams torment me? Why does longing fill me—useless, hopeless longing for some fairy-tale world where it would all have been different?

A world in which Haughton was hers. In which Max was hers.

But what was the point of such longings? What would be the point, now, in standing here in the cold wind, in this alien land, and dreading a future on her own, without Haughton, without Max? What would be the point of admitting that what she had tried to pass off as merely a predictable reaction to the first man in her life was so much more?

What would be the point in admitting she'd fallen in love with him?

Max turned the powerful car on to the long curve of the gravelled drive, flanked at either side by a crimson blaze of rhododendrons, misted with bluebells along its verges, until the vista opened up to reveal the lawns and gardens beyond, and then the house itself, with the pale mauve of wisteria coming into bloom tumbling over the porch.

Haughton was, indeed, looking its best in the late spring sunshine. Satisfaction overflowed in him.

He had achieved exactly what he wanted, and as he parked his car in the kitchen courtyard his mind went back to the first time he had done so.

I fell in love with this place the moment I saw it and nothing has changed.

Except that Haughton was now his.

Satisfaction curved his mouth into a smile, putting a gleam into his dark eyes as he strode up to the back door. Haughton was *his*. His to do exactly as he wanted! With no more blocks or obstacles or impediments.

His keys were at the ready—after the completion of his purchase they were in his possession—and he unlocked the back door, glancing briefly into the kitchen where Ellen had hurled at his head her refusal to sell her share of the property unless it was forced from her by a court of law. Yet again satisfaction filled him. Well, that had not proved necessary.

He walked down the stone-flagged corridor to push open the green baize door and walk out into the front hall. It was chilly there, with no heating on yet, but that would be easily remedied. He paused, and gazed around, feeling the silence of the old house lap at him.

It's waiting. Waiting for its new owner to take possession. To live here and make a home here. To love it as it wants to be loved, to cherish it and value it.

Into his head came the memory of how he'd stood on this very spot, recognising his self-discovery, his sudden determination that he should make a home here for himself—recalling the moment he'd first felt that overpowering urge so strongly.

For a fleeting moment regret showed in his eyes for what he had done. Then it was gone. He had done what he had done, and it was what he had wanted to do. He would allow himself to feel nothing but satisfaction at having accomplished it. Nothing but that. He would have no regrets at how he had achieved it—at the price that had been paid for it. None.

He strode to the front door, throwing back the bolts and locks and opening it wide. Only one more signature was required to fulfil his purpose, to achieve what he wanted to do. And that would be supplied soon—very soon. He stood and watched over the gardens. Waiting...

Ellen sat in the back of the taxi taking her from the station to Haughton. A grief so profound she could not name its depth filled her. This was to be her very last time walking into the house that had been her home—that was hers no longer. Now, after landing that morning from Toronto, her charges having been safely bestowed upon their waiting parents, she was coming here only to remove her own personal possessions and the few keepsakes she still had from her parents before returning to Canada.

Everything else was included in the sale. A sale that had been conducted at breakneck speed the moment she'd made that fatal phone call to her solicitor to yield victory to Pauline and Chloe.

Now all that remained was for her to put her

signature to the contract. She'd be calling in at the family solicitor on her way back to the station. Where Pauline and Chloe were she did not know and did not care. They'd signed the contract and taken themselves off—presumably to await the transfer of their share of the sale price into their accounts and then spend it as lavishly on themselves as they had spent all the rest of her father's money.

She closed her eyes. She must not let bitterness and anger fill her again. *She must not!* Max had been right—those harsh emotions had eaten away at her for too long. Now she had to make a new life for herself. A life without Haughton. A life without Max.

She felt her throat constrict, felt pain lance at her.

I've lost my home and I've lost my heart as well. I can bear neither of them, and yet I must.

'Stop! Please!'

The words broke from her as the taxi driver turned between the stone pillars on to the drive. Startled, he braked, and Ellen fumbled for money, pressing it into his hand and scrambling from the vehicle.

Dragging her pull-along suitcase behind her, she started along the drive. Emotion poured through her, agonising and unbearable, a storm of feelings clutched at her heart. Soon…oh, *so* soon…all that would be left to her of her beloved home would be memories.

I was happy here once. And no one can take those memories from me. Wherever I go in the world I will take them with me.

She took a searing breath. Just as she would take the memories of her time with Max—that brief, precious time with him.

I had Haughton for a quarter of a century and I had Max for only weeks. But the memories of both must last my lifetime.

An ache started in her so profound it suffused her whole being with a longing and a desire for all that she had lost—the home she had lost, the man she had lost.

As the massed rhododendrons in their crimson glory gave way to lawn she plunged across the grass, cutting up towards the house, her eyes going immediately to its frontage.

This is the last time I shall see it! The last time…the very last time! The last time—

She stopped dead. There, standing on the porch, was a figure—tall and dominating and already in full possession.

It was Max.

Max watched her approach. He'd timed his own arrival perfectly, having obtained from her school details of the flight she'd be on, and calculating how long it would take her to reach here. He had the paperwork all ready.

As she reached the porch he could see her face was white, the skin stretched tight over her features. He felt emotion pierce him, but suppressed it. No time for that now. He must complete this business as swiftly as possible.

'What are you doing here?' The question broke from Ellen even though the moment it was out she knew how stupid it was. What was he doing here? He was taking possession—as he had every right to do.

His long lashes dipped down over his eyes. 'Waiting for you,' he said.

He stood aside, gesturing for her to step into the house.

His house. That's what it is now. Not mine—

not once I've completed the final step that I must take and put my signature on the contract for my share. That's all he is waiting for now.

She swallowed. Anguish seared her. Dear God, why did he have to be here? Why must she endure this final ordeal?

How can I bear it?

How could she bear to see him again? How could she bear to feel that terrifying leap in her pulse, which had soared the moment her eyes had lit on him? How could she bear to have her gaze latch on to him, to drink him in like a quenching fountain after a parched desert?

He was crossing to the door to the library. 'Come,' he said to her, 'I have the paperwork here.'

Numbly she followed him, her suitcase abandoned on the porch. She was incapable of thought. Incapable of anything except letting her eyes cling to his form. She felt weak with it—weak with the shock of seeing him again. Weak with the emotion surging in her as she looked at him.

He went to her father's desk and she could see the documents set out on it. He indicated the chair and, zombie-like, she went to sit on it, her legs like straw suddenly.

She looked at him across the desk. 'I was going to do this at the solicitor's later today,' she said. Her voice sounded dazed.

He gave a quick shake of his head. 'No need,' he said, and picked up the pen next to the paper-work, holding it out to her.

Ellen took a breath, ready to sign. What else could she do?

Do it—just do it now. It has to be done, has to be faced, has to be endured. Just as seeing him again has to be endured.

She lowered the pen to the paper. Then, abruptly, before she could start to write, she stopped. The enormity of what she was about to do had frozen her.

She lifted her head to stare helplessly up at Max.

'Ellen—sign the contract. Go on—sign it.'

There was something implacable in his face now. Something that made her eyes search his features. Something, she realised, that was mak-ing her flinch inwardly. Making her forcibly aware that this was a man who dealt in multimillion-pound deals as casually as he ordered a bottle of vintage wine. That to him this purchase was nothing but small fry—a drop in the ocean—when it was the whole ocean itself to her.

Did he see the flash of anguish in her eyes, hear the low catch of her breath—suspect the emotion stabbing at her now? She didn't know…knew only that he had placed both his hands, palms down, on the edge of the desk opposite her, that his tall frame was looming over her. Dominating, purposeful.

She tried to remember how different he could be—how he had stood at the helm of that catamaran, facing into the wind, his dark hair tousled, his smile lighting up the world for her. How laughter had shaken his shoulders as they'd laughed at something absurd that had caught his humour. How his dark eyes had blazed with fierce desire as he'd swept her into his arms and lowered his possessing mouth to hers…

'Just sign,' he said again, wiping all the anguished memories from her. His eyes bored into hers. 'It's for your own good,' he said.

His voice was soft, but there was a weight of intent in it that pressed upon her.

She lowered her head, breaking the crushing gaze that was bending her to his will. His words echoed hollowly. Forcing her to accept their truth. The truth as he saw it—the truth as he had made *her* see it. She could not go on as she had sought to do, locked in a toxic, unwinnable power struggle in the bitter aftermath of her father's death.

Slowly, carefully, she set her signature to the document before her, on the final page of it. The only clause visible was full of incomprehensible legal jargon she did not bother to read. Then, swallowing, she sheathed the pen and put it down. It was done—finally done. She had no claim on what had once been her home. Now it was just one more property in Max Vasilikos's investment portfolio.

Emotion twisted inside her. Impulsively she spoke. 'Max! Please…I know that the future of Haughton is nothing to do with me…' She swallowed and her voice changed, becoming imploring. 'But this was once a happy family home. Please—think how it could be so again!'

She saw a veil come down over his eyes. He straightened, took a step away, glanced around the room they were in. The original dark panelling was still there, and the serried ranks of books, the smoke-stained fireplace with its hearthrug and her father's worn leather chair. Then his eyes came back to her.

'When I first came to Haughton,' he said slowly, 'my plan, if I decided to buy it, was to realise the value in it and likely sell it on, or rent it out for revenue. But...' His eyes flickered to the tall windows, out over the gardens beyond, then moved back to her again. 'But as I walked around, saw it for myself, I realised that I did not want that.'

He looked at her. His expression was still veiled, but there was something behind that veil that caught at her, though she did not know why.

'I realised,' he said slowly, and now a different note had entered his voice, 'that I wanted to keep this house for myself. That I wanted to make this house my home.'

He looked at her. The veil was impenetrable now, and yet she gazed at him fixedly still.

'I still want that—for it to be a home,' he said.

For just a fraction of a moment his eyes met hers. Then she pulled her eyes away, closing them tightly. Emotion was sweeping up in her.

'I'm glad.' Her voice was tight with emotion.

'Oh, Max, I'm glad!' Her eyes flew open again. 'It deserves to be loved and cherished, to be a happy home again.'

There was a catch in her voice, a catch in her heart. To hear that this was what Max wanted—that Haughton would be protected from the fate she'd dreaded for it—was wonderful! And yet her heart ached to know that he would make a home here for himself…only for himself.

Until one day he brings his wife here!

Images forced themselves upon her. Max carrying his bride over the threshold, sweeping her up the stairs…his threshold, his stairs, his bride. Max running effortlessly on untired limbs around the pathway beside the lake, taking in his domain, making it his own. Max surrounded one day by children—a Christmas tree here in this hall, where she had once opened her childhood presents—their laughter echoing as hers had once done.

Max's children. Max's bride and Max's wife. Max's home.

And she would be in Canada, or any place in the world. For where she was would not matter—

could not matter. Because she would be without Haughton.

Without Max.

Pain lanced at her and she got to her feet, scraping her father's chair on the floorboards. She faced Max. He was still standing there, his expression still veiled, still resting his gaze on her.

'Yes,' he said. 'It does. It does deserve that.'

He spoke the words heavily, incisively, as if they were being carved into him. He looked at her, held her eyes unreadably for one last moment longer, then spoke again.

'And I hope beyond all things that it will be *my* home—'

She stared at him. Why had he said that? It *was* his home now—her signature had made it so.

But he was speaking still. 'That, however, depends entirely on you.'

Bewilderment filled her. There was something in his eyes now—something that, had the sombreness and the despair of the moment not overwhelmed her, she would have said was a glint.

'You should always read what you're signing before you sign it, Ellen,' he said softly, and his eyes were still holding hers.

'It's a contract of sale,' she said.

Her voice was neutral, but she was trying desperately in her head not to hear the seductive, sensuous echo of his naming of her, that had sent a thousand dangerous whispers across her skin.

'Yes, it is,' he agreed.

'Selling you my share of Haughton.'

'No,' said Max, in measured, deliberate tones. 'It is not that.' He paused. 'Read it—you've signed it…now read it.'

Numbly, she turned back the pages to reach the opening page. But it was full of legalese and jargon, and the words swam in front of her eyes.

Then Max was speaking again. 'It *is* a contract of sale,' he said, 'but *you* are not the vendor.' He paused. 'I am.'

CHAPTER TWELVE

Max's eyes were holding hers and not letting them go—not letting them go for an instant...a single second.

'You see...' he said, and he spoke in the same measured tones, but now there was something else in his voice—something that was an emotion rising up to break through, an emotion that was possessing every cell in his body. 'You see, I am selling you the two-thirds share of Haughton I have already purchased from your stepmother and stepsister. Which, Ellen—' and now the emotion broke through finally, unstoppably, blazing through him, lighting up his eyes with the fire he had banked down with every ounce of his strength since he'd watched her walk up to him across the lawns '—which I now restore to *you*.'

For one last moment he held on to his self-control.

'I've given you a very good price,' he told her. 'I believe even on your teacher's salary you can afford to pay me a hundred pounds. How does that sound? I hope it's acceptable—because you've just put your signature to it.'

She wasn't saying anything. She was just staring at him as incomprehension, shock, disbelief, all flashed across her face.

'I don't understand...' It was a whisper, faint and scarcely audible.

For one long, timeless, endless moment the tableau held. Max standing there, his face expressionless, and she seated across the desk from him, as white as a sheet with shock etched across her features. Then, like a dam breaking, all the emotions Max had been holding in check burst from him.

'Did you truly think I would take your home from you—after you'd ripped the scales from my eyes?'

He took a shuddering breath, making himself calm. His gaze was on her, holding her like a magnet.

'The moment you hurled what you did at me, before you stormed out, I knew there was only one thing to do. Only one! And now...' A sigh of profound relief went through him. 'Now it's done. I put my legal team on to it straight away, the minute you'd gone, and they got hold of your stepmother out in Spain and told her I'd buy their share even without yours.'

A hard, cynical look entered his eyes.

'She jumped at the chance like I was dangling a diamond necklace in front of her. My lawyer phoned me their agreement when I was in the Gulf, and then I knew, finally, that I was free to do what I have just done.' He paused, and an expression moved across his face that showed all that had possessed him until this moment, the driving urgency to accomplish what he had. 'Make Haughton safe for you,' he finished.

She heard him, yet still she dared not believe what he was saying. Dared not believe that she had just bought her beloved home back for herself—for a song—for a gift...

For of course it *was* a gift! How could it be otherwise at so paltry a price? A gift that Max had given her—a gift so wonderful, so precious that it took her breath away, squeezed her lungs so tight she could hardly breathe, could hardly feel the beating of her heart, though it was hammering in her chest.

'Why?' It was the only word she could say, as faint and low as her breath could make it. 'Max— *why*?'

She took a searing breath through the constriction in her throat and made herself speak again, forced the words from her though they were still low and faint.

'Why should you care what Pauline and Chloe did to my father and me? Why should you give me so fabulous a gift?'

He was looking at her still, and the expression in his face made the hammering in her heart pound in her ears.

'Why?'

His voice echoed hers. But he gave her no answer. Only strode around her father's desk, catching at her hand and drawing her to her feet. Her legs were like jelly and she had to cling to his arm lest she collapse, so overpowering was the shock shaking her.

In her head she kept hearing her own voice,

saying over and over again—*Haughton is mine! It's mine! It's mine! Dear God, it's mine for ever now!*

It was a paean, an anthem, ringing in her head like bells. She gazed helplessly up at Max. At the man who had done this, made this happen. Into her head, flashing like a strobe light, came the memory of the moment Max had given her that first wonderful, miraculous gift—the moment when he'd shown her her reflection the night of the ball, transformed beyond recognition. Made beautiful by him.

He freed me from Chloe's hex—and now, oh, he's freed me from Pauline's too!

Emotion overwhelmed her. Gratitude and wonder and so much more.

'Why?' His voice came again, husky now. He caught her other hand, held it, cherished it. He towered over her, his strong body supporting her stricken one. 'Oh, Ellen—my beautiful, lovely, passionate, wonderful Ellen... Have you really not the faintest idea why?'

He held her a little way from him, the expression on his face rueful.

'Did you not hear me when I told you that the

moment I saw this house I wanted to live here? That something about it called to me? That after all my years of wandering, never having had a home of my own, having existed only on sufferance at my stepfather's *taverna* and having lived in hotels and apartments anywhere in the world, I had finally come across a place that urged me to stop…to stop and stay. Make my life here.'

Now the rueful expression deepened.

'That was what drove me so hard to buy it—to make it mine. What drove me to do all I could to achieve that aim. Including…' his eyes met hers wryly '…whisking you off to London to show you how good your life could be if only you would let go of the place I wanted for myself.'

He gave a regretful sigh.

'I went on and on at you. I know I did. But you see…' and now a different note entered his voice '…I'd sought an explanation for your stubbornness, your refusal to agree to sell your share, from your stepmother and stepsister.' His eyes shadowed as he remembered that scene in the drawing room when he'd made his initial offer for Haughton. 'And they told me that you'd become obsessed with the house, that you'd never

accepted Pauline's marriage to your father, that
you had rejected them from the very first, seen
them as interlopers, invaders.'

He gave a shake of his head.

'I remembered my own childhood—how my
stepfather never wanted me, never accepted me
into his home, always resented my presence even
though he made use of it. I was always the out-
sider, the unwanted brat of my mother. Maybe,'
he said slowly, 'that was why I was so ready
to believe what Pauline and Chloe told me. So,
while I could make allowances for your reaction
to your father's remarriage, all I could see was
how that resentment was poisoning you…chain-
ing you to this place. Making you think it was the
only way you could punish Pauline for marrying
your father, seeking to take your mother's place.'

He felt Ellen draw away slightly. Her eyes were
full of grief. Her voice when she spoke was low
and strained, her glance going to her father's
empty chair by the hearth.

'I was *glad* when my father told me he was
marrying again. So glad! He'd been grieving for
my mother and I desperately wanted him to be
happy again. If Pauline made him happy, then I

knew I would be happy. I tried to welcome them, tried to befriend Chloe...' A choke broke in her voice. 'Well, I told you how they reacted. But even then if they'd only made my father happy I could have borne it! But within months of marrying Pauline my father realised that her only interest in him was his money.'

Her mouth set.

'He was powerless to do anything about it. If he'd divorced Pauline she'd have taken half of everything he had—forced him to sell Haughton and split the proceeds. So he kept on paying out and paying out and paying out. I had to hide from him all the spite and venom that came from them—hide from him how Chloe had tried to make my life hell at school, and how she constantly sneered at me because I'm tall and sporty, told me how repellent I was because of it until I believed her completely...'

Her voice broke in another choke before she could continue.

'I had to hide it all from my father because he'd only have been hurt all the more, worried about me more, and felt yet more trapped by Pauline. So when he died I was almost relieved, because finally I didn't have to pretend any longer. I could find my backbone and resolve that even though I knew it was impossible to stop Pauline and Chloe from getting their claws into Haughton eventually I would do everything in my power, for as long as I could, to make it as hard and as expensive as possible for them to force a sale.'

She took another choking breath.

'I was—just as you said—using Haughton as a weapon against them—my only weapon.' Her gaze shifted again, became shadowed. 'But when I came back here after leaving you I knew...' She paused, then made herself go on. 'I knew that I'd changed—that you'd been right to say that I was poisoning myself in my battle against them. That it was time...finally time...to let go. They had won and I had lost and all I could do was leave and make a new life for myself somewhere else. *Anywhere* else.' She took another searing, painful breath. 'This—today—was to be my very last visit, my last sight of my home.'

He drew her towards him again and his voice was gentle...very gentle. 'And now it is yours for ever.' His eyes poured into hers. 'No one can ever threaten it again.' His mouth curved into a smile. 'Look around you, Ellen—it's yours, all yours.'

A strangled sound was torn from her throat, and then a sob, and then another, and then tears were spilling from her eyes and Max was wrapping his arms around her, and she was clinging to him, shaking with emotion, with the relief and disbelief that all this was really true, that all the stress and fear and anguish at losing her home was over—over for ever. Because Max—wonderful, kind, generous Max—had made her dream come true. Haughton was hers, and it was safe for ever now.

He held her while her body shook with the tears choking from her, convulsing her, while her hands clutched at him and she was finally purged of all that her stepmother and stepsister had done to her for so long. And when she was finally done he stroked her hair with his hand, murmured things to her in Greek.

She didn't know what they were, but knew that he was the most wonderful man on earth. And that she had now taken from him something he had wanted from the moment he'd first set eyes on it.

Her thoughts whirled in her head, troubling her. She lifted her face from his shoulder, looked up at him with an anxious look.

'Max, I still don't understand. You've given me this miraculous gift and I still don't understand *why*. Why would you do it when you've told me yourself that you fell in love with Haughton and wanted to make your home here? How can you bear to give it away to me like this?'

He looked down at her, his deep, dark eyes holding an expression she could not recognise.

'Well, you see, Ellen, I'm forced to admit that I am a shamefully devious character.' He cradled her to him, his hands resting loosely around her spine. '*Shamefully* devious. Yes, it's absolutely true that I was…devastated…' his voice was edgy suddenly '…when I realised how wrong I'd been about you—about your behaviour towards Pauline and Chloe over this house—how deceived I'd been by their appearance of solicitude towards you, how disgusted I felt at their exploitation of your father and their cruelty to you. It made me absolutely determined to redress this final wrong, to restore your home to you, out of their clutches. But…'

His voice changed again, softening now, taking on a hint of wry humour.

'But even while I was set on being the one to save Haughton for you, because you love it so much and have been through so much because of it, I also knew perfectly well that I had... Well, let's say an ulterior motive all along.'

There was a glint in his eyes now, blatantly visible. It did things to Ellen's insides that even the flood of emotion over regaining her home could not quench—things that took her back instantly to the time she'd spent with Max abroad, setting loose a quiver inside her, a quickening of her pulse that made her all too aware of how Max's body was cradling hers, of the lean strength of him, the taut wall of his chest, the pressure of his hips, the heat of his body...

'I told you when you signed my contract restoring Haughton to you how much I was still hoping to make it my home,' he was saying now, 'but that it would depend entirely on you. So...' He raised a quizzical eyebrow. 'What do you think? Could you bear to share Haughton with me?'

She looked at him, not understanding. 'Do you mean some kind of co-ownership?' she ventured.

He shook his head. 'No, I don't want you ever to have to worry about not owning Haughton one hundred per cent,' he said. 'I was *thinking*,' he went on, and now the glint was even more pronounced, and she felt a sudden tightening of the arms around her spine, 'of a *different* way to make this my home.'

'I don't understand...' she said again. But her voice was weaker this time. Her whole body was weaker.

'Then maybe,' said Max, 'this will make things clearer.'

He let her go suddenly, and she felt herself leaning back on the desk as his hold on her was relinquished. She clutched the edge of the desk with her hands. Saw him reach into his jacket, draw out a tiny square box. Felt her heart rate slow...slow almost to a standstill. The breath in her lungs was congealing.

Before her very eyes she saw him lower himself upon one knee and look back up at her.

'Will you...?' he said, and his eyes pinioned hers as she gazed down at him, her own eyes widening until they could widen no further. 'Will you, my most beautiful, most wonderful, most lovely and fit and fabulous and incomparable Ellen, do me the honour, the very *great* honour, of making me the happiest of men? Will you…?' he asked. 'Will you marry me?'

He flicked open the box and her eyes went to the flash of red within. She gave a gasp.

Max quirked an eyebrow again. 'I'm sort of hoping,' he said, 'again quite shamelessly, that this might help persuade you.'

He took the ring out, got to his feet, lifted Ellen's nerveless left hand and held it. His other hand held the ring. The ring she'd worn at the Edwardian ball that had changed her life for ever. The ring that had been her mother's engagement ring, given to her by her father. The ring that had once belonged to her grandmother and her great-grandmother.

'How did you get it…?' Her voice was faint again.

'I bought the ruby parure you wore to the ball. And by the same token I also bought back all your mother's jewellery that Pauline and Chloe helped themselves to—it was in the fine print of the terms and conditions of their sale contract. As for everything else—all the other jewellery and antiques and paintings they sold—I've got a team searching them out and I will buy them all back as and when we find them.' And now that glint was blatant again. 'You see, Ellen, I want to do absolutely everything in my power to persuade you to do what I want you to do more than anything else in the world—and, my sweet Ellen, you haven't actually answered me yet.'

Was there tension in his voice, lacing through the humour, turning the glint in his eyes to something very different?

She gazed at him. Her heart was suddenly in her throat—or something was. Something huge and choking that was making it quite impossible for her to do anything at all except gaze at him. And force out one breathless whisper.

'Did…did you just propose to me?' she asked faintly.

A tidal wave of disbelief was sweeping up through her—the same as when he'd told her he'd gifted his newly acquired share of Haughton to her.

A rasp broke from Max. 'Do you want a replay?' he said, and he started to go down on his knee again.

She snatched at him to stop him. 'No! No—*no*!'

He halted, looked at her quizzically. 'Is that no, you won't marry me?' he asked her.

She shook her head violently. She could not speak. Emotion was pounding her, crashing in on her consciousness, overwhelming her.

'So, that's a yes, then, is it?' Max pursued. He paused. 'I'd just like to clarify this, if you don't mind. Because it is, you see, somewhat important to me.' His expression changed suddenly. 'It's going to determine my entire future happiness.'

She swallowed. That huge, choking lump was still in her throat, and the tidal wash of emotion was still pounding in her.

'Why...?' The single word was faint, uncomprehending.

'Why, what?' he said blankly.

His self-control was under the greatest pressure he'd ever experienced in his life. Even worse than that very first night of the revelation of her beauty to him, when she had offered her mouth to him and he had swooped upon it with all the hunger of a starving man—and then, with the feast before him, had had to draw back, let her go and get the hell out of her bedroom before he'd succumbed to the most intense temptation he'd ever known.

Even worse than that…

'Why…?' She swallowed. 'Why are you asking me to marry you?'

And Max lost it. Finally lost it. It had all been just too damn much. Too damn much from the moment Ellen had laid into him in his hotel suite, telling him the truth about the vultures who were feeding off her. In that single instant he'd known exactly what he was going to do—and he'd spent the last fortnight pulling out every stop, racing to get the paperwork done, the contracts drawn up and completed, and to drive down here to do what he had just done. Hand her back her home and gain her for himself.

'Will *this* help you understand?' he demanded.

He swept her up to him, his strength easily crushing her against him, his mouth swooping down on hers. And instantly she went up in flames, her mouth opening to his, melding with his. Her arms wound around him, her fingers spearing into his hair. She was hungry for him. Desperate for him. When finally he released her she was shaking, breathless.

Max's hands splayed around her face. 'I've fallen in love with you,' he said.

His voice was quiet but there was an intensity in it, a strength that came from the very core of his being.

'Somewhere along the way I've fallen in love with you. Oh, I admit that my motives in taking you to London were entirely self-interested—you knew that…knew I was seeking to open your eyes to what your life could be like beyond the narrow confines you'd imprisoned yourself in with your vendetta against your stepmother and stepsister once you'd discovered your own beauty. But once I'd discovered it too—and helped myself to it!' His voice was wry. 'Once I'd whisked you off to enjoy it to the full… Well…' Warmth infused his voice now. 'It dawned on me that I was enjoying your company in a way I'd never experienced with any other woman.'

'Even Tyla Brentley?' Ellen breathed.

A dismissive sound came from his throat. 'Tyla was lovely to look at, glamorous to be with—and totally self-absorbed. You… Ah, *you* were utterly different. Even before you had your makeover I knew that. You're intelligent, clear-sighted, and

I approve of your efforts with all those deprived city children.'

He dropped a kiss on her nose.

'We had a good time together, Ellen, on our travels. We were good together—incredibly, fantastically good. And when you stormed off I wasn't just appalled to discover how vicious your step-relations were, I also knew I desperately didn't want you to leave me! I knew I *had* to try and get you back—get you back so we could go on being good together. Good together for the rest of our lives, Ellen—that's what I so hope for.'

Something changed in his voice again now, and an urgency speared it.

'And if somewhere along the way you happen... just happen to come to feel for me what I feel for you... Well...'

She didn't let him finish. She reached up her hand, snaked it around the back of his head, hauled his mouth down to hers again. She pressed her lips hard against him to silence him. Then, as she drew back again, emotion burst in her.

And so did a storm of weeping.

For the second time in a handful of minutes she clutched at him as wave after wave of emotion swept through her yet again—and again and again. Max loved her—he *loved* her! He'd given her the inestimable gift of her home to her, and he'd given her a more incomparable gift as well.

Himself. His heart. His love.

'Max! Oh, Max!' It was all she could say. But it seemed to satisfy him.

As she finally came down on the other side of the tsunami inside her he patted her back and reached for the ring box, sitting abandoned on her father's desk.

'That's *got* to be a definite yes,' he told her, with satisfaction in his voice and the love in his eyes pouring out over her, embracing her and caressing her.

'Of *course* it is!' She gulped. 'I kept telling my-self that because you were the first man in my life of course I'd get the idea in my head that I'd fallen in love with you—but it wasn't just that. It was real. Completely real what I was feeling for you. When I stormed out on you it was tearing me to pieces, and being out in Canada, facing the rest of my life without Haughton and with-out *you*—I…I just couldn't bear it!'

Tears threatened again, spilling into her watery eyes.

'And now I've got both—I've got my beloved home and I've got something even more desperately precious to me.' Her face worked. 'I've got *you*. And you, my dearest, most adored and most *wonderful* Max, are my heart, my life—the love of my life.'

'Excellent!' he said, and his satisfaction was total now. 'So,' he said to her, taking the ruby ring from its case, 'do we finally get to the ring bit now?'

He took her hand again and, not waiting for an answer, slid the ring carefully over her finger. But he did not relinquish her hand. Instead he gazed down at her.

'When I first walked into this house I knew it was the place I wanted to call my home,' he told her. His face was serious now—completely serious. 'I had a sudden vision...a vision of myself here, with the woman I love, making our home here together, raising our family here together.' His eyes had a rueful glint in them again. 'I thought that I would have to bring her here, having found her somewhere out in the world beyond. And yet all along—' His voice changed, and there was a crack in it, he knew. 'All along she was here. Waiting for me to find her. Waiting,' he said, 'to find *me*.'

He paused minutely.

'And now,' he said, 'we're done with waiting. Done with finding. We can just enjoy, Ellen. Enjoy the rest of our lives together.'

His mouth lowered to hers and he kissed her softly, gently, before withdrawing. He felt her fingers tightening over his as his lips brushed hers, felt the sudden constricting of her throat, saw the misting of her eyes as he drew his head away.

'So…' he said, because he wanted to make sure—to make absolutely, totally sure of his future happiness…a happiness that was already flooding through him, soaking through every cell in his body, radiating from him like a beacon. 'Have we finally got everything sorted? I love you, you love me, and we're going to marry and live here together in this house we both love, make it a home again, for you and for me and for all the children we are most definitely going to have! A happy family home for a happy family—just as we both wanted. Did I leave anything out?' he asked.

Ellen leaned into his shoulder. Her sigh was pure happiness. 'No,' she said. 'I think you've just described heaven on earth.'

Max smiled. A warm, approving smile that melted her all the way through.

'That's what I thought,' he said. He dropped another kiss on her nose. 'I do like to be right,' he told her.

He straightened up.

'OK, it's a lovely day—actually the best day in my entire life so far—let's get outdoors. Let's get into the sunshine—the sunshine of our lives, my adored, beautiful goddess and lioness.'

She looked at him. 'Can I be *both*?' she queried, with a teasing smile in her eyes.

Max's mouth quirked, his expression doting. 'You can be everything you want, my beloved, providing you go on loving me.'

He started to lead the way out of the library and across the hall, his hand wound in hers and hers in his. Side by side and shoulder to shoulder.

'And you me,' said Ellen.

He paused at the door. 'Deal,' said Max, and kissed her once again.

Then, with a squeeze of her hand, he opened the front door and they stepped through it, into the sunshine, into the happiness of their life together, into their love for each other.

EPILOGUE

MAX WRAPPED HIS arm around Ellen and drew her closer against his shoulder as they leant back against the sun-warmed stone. They were sitting on the step of the little folly, looking out over the lake to where the setting sun was turning its reedy waters bronze. Ellen gave a sigh of deep contentment as she nestled into Max's sheltering embrace, her knees drawn up and slanting against his thighs.

'You're really sure you're OK with us spending our honeymoon here at Haughton?' she asked him, glancing up at his profile.

He nodded, his gaze going to her. 'My beautiful, adored Ellen—don't you know that I am happy wherever *you* are? And if you are happiest here, then here we shall stay for all our days,' Max finished with a fond smile, and let his lips brush across her hair.

'Maybe,' she mused, 'I feel that if I ever leave

Haughton I'll return to find that this heaven was only a dream, and I'm back here again with Pauline and Chloe still trying to sell it from under my feet and force me out,' she said.

Max shook his head. 'Oh, no,' he said decisively. 'This heaven is real, believe me. And as for your stepmother and stepsister—well, they'll never set foot on your property again, I promise you. If they even come back to the UK I'll know about it!'

She looked at him quizzically. 'Are you really keeping them under surveillance?' she asked.

'I'm keeping tabs on them, yes,' Max admitted. 'So that wherever in the world they go, if they try and home in on anyone wealthy but vulnerable, like your father was, then their target will be warned. Of course,' he went on, 'it could be that they won't need to target money any more—they have pots of their own. And I don't mean just their ill-gotten gains from selling me their share of Haughton!'

Ellen's quizzical look intensified and Max elucidated.

'I just happened to mention to them, at some point while I was acquiring their share of Haughton, several new property hotspots that were emerging, where substantial profits could be made. They seized on it, and my latest information is that they're now investing substantially. However, if they're prudent they'll take on board that where there is the chance of high return there's also the chance of being wiped out financially.' He smiled, and it was not a wholly benign smile. 'Let's just say that if they *do* get wiped out financially...well, I for one will not be weeping.'

Ellen looked away, out over the lake. She had come so close to losing her beloved home that it was hard to feel any concern at the prospect of Pauline and Chloe losing the money they'd made on selling up to the man who'd saved Haughton for her.

'Karma,' she murmured now.

'Yes, indeed,' agreed Max. 'And it was fate, too, that brought me here...let me find you here.'

He turned his head to look across the lake, beyond the lawns, to the mellow stone house that was now home to both of them, safe and secure for ever, for themselves and for their children to come. Contentment filled him. With his free hand he reached sideways to lift the bottle of champagne from its ice bucket.

'Time for a refill,' he said, and Ellen picked up

her empty glass and held it tilted while he topped it up, then held his glass while he did likewise.

He set down the champagne bottle and raised his brimming glass, clinking it against hers.

'This is to us,' he said, and now his eyes wound into hers, his love for her glowing like an eternal flame. 'To our marriage, to our lives together, to our love—and to our beautiful, most precious home.'

'To us,' she echoed. 'To you, my darling, wonderful Max, who has made all my dreams come true!'

He dropped a kiss on her upturned face, then took a deep draught of champagne as she did likewise.

'It's going to be quite a busy honeymoon,' he observed. '*Un*decorating the house from all that interior design, getting it back to the way it used to be… It's great,' he added, 'that so much of the original furniture got stashed in the attics.'

'We *will* need new curtains, though, and soft furnishings,' Ellen commented.

'We'll choose them together. Did I tell you?' He cast a wicked look at his bride. 'I've always had a thing about spots. I think curtains made from a polka dot fabric would be ideal…' He trailed off.

She laughed. 'Let's save that for the nursery, maybe,' she said.

He cast her an interested look. 'Are you trying to tell me something?'

His voice was casual, but Ellen was not deceived.

'Well, no,' she admitted. 'But maybe this time next year? That should give my headmistress time to sort out maternity cover.'

'You really want to go on teaching?' Max asked.

'Oh, yes,' she answered. 'I can't just be the idle wife of a rich man! And besides…' it was her turn to throw him a wicked look '…if I don't teach Games I might go off the boil about exercise in general. I might run to fat,' she said dulcetly. 'And *then*,' she finished dramatically, 'you wouldn't love me any more!'

A growl came from Max and he set down his champagne glass, removing hers at the same time. His arm around her shoulder tightened, and with his free hand he cupped her face.

'My goddess—my lioness—you could turn into a morbidly obese rhinoceros and I wouldn't love you an iota less. Don't you realise it's *you* I love, and to hell with anything else?'

'Oh, Max!' She gave a little choke, feeling her eyes misting suddenly.

How blessed she was—how unutterably blessed—that Max should love her!

He kissed her, warm and tender, deep and passionate.

Increasingly passionate.

Gently he drew her down upon the stone floor of the folly, and their bodies were limned with the light of the setting sun as desire flared between them—rich and ardent, sweet and eternal. Desire that was the manifestation of a love that would not end—that *could* not end. That could only bind them, each to the other, all their days…

* * * * *

If you enjoyed this story, don't miss these other great reads from Julia James

A TYCOON TO BE RECKONED WITH
CAPTIVATED BY THE GREEK
THE FORBIDDEN TOUCH OF SANGUARDO
SECURING THE GREEK'S LEGACY
PAINTED THE OTHER WOMAN

Available now!

MILLS & BOON®
Large Print – February 2017

The Return of the Di Sione Wife
Caitlin Crews

Baby of His Revenge
Jennie Lucas

The Spaniard's Pregnant Bride
Maisey Yates

A Cinderella for the Greek
Julia James

Married for the Tycoon's Empire
Abby Green

Indebted to Moreno
Kate Walker

A Deal with Alejandro
Maya Blake

A Mistletoe Kiss with the Boss
Susan Meier

A Countess for Christmas
Christy McKellen

Her Festive Baby Bombshell
Jennifer Faye

The Unexpected Holiday Gift
Sophie Pembroke